CW01203200

Voices in the Mirror

By Ross Turner

Noemi/

Congratulations!

Thank you for entering.

Enjoy!

Ross/

Ross Turner

©Ross Turner

Because life is so much smaller than I used to think it was,

Because all things, both good and bad, eventually come around, and because all things, both good and bad, eventually end,

Always,

Ross.

It is perhaps not the Church and all that it stands for that some fear so, but instead the demons of humanity that lurk within, tainting its Holy walls with their evil and their lust and their malice.

And what if that window into our own souls wasn't just to show us our reflections, the good and bad of who we are, but instead the reflection of the whole world around us, and how we see that, in all its entirety of good and evil.

Chapter One

"Though at times, my friends, I know it may feel like it's all too much: like there's simply no way to handle the difficult days. But I assure you, with all my heart, that there are always better times ahead."

Father Peter's voice echoed around the vast church almost endlessly, and had a ring of both finality and fate to it as he began to round up his Service for that morning.

He was not an overly tall man, and though past the age of fifty years, he had a head full of hair that looked as though it belonged to a much younger fellow, albeit frosted silver by the sometimes not so delicate hands of time.

"The demons that haunt you today, will be your liberation tomorrow. This I can sorely promise you."

Despite his relatively small stature and stocky frame, garbed in a long, dark robe tied loosely at the waist, Father Peter had the uncanny ability to hold an enormous presence over anybody whom he held in council.

By no means was this because he was an intimidating figure, not by any stretch of the imagination. Far from it in fact.

Instead, it was simply because he held himself with an almost unworldly aura and presence, something rarely found amongst mankind, and even more rarely found amongst those decent ones among us.

It was not only that, but also his seemingly inhuman and unfaltering positivity that stood Father Peter aside from the rest. Such qualities, naturally, made him the first port of call for anyone in need that called the village home. The whole of Riverbrook attended his Services, and without fail they always left feeling much more optimistic than when they arrived, and that was all and more that Father Peter could ask for.

The church itself was a long, tall building, constructed with unimaginably large stone blocks. Set high in the walls with only five or six paces between each of them, were large stained glass windows, each depicting an angel or a demon or some such scene from a moral-strewn tale, each designed to inspire and stir the eye of their beholder in one way or another.

Light streamed in through the windows in a vast array of stained colours, for it was a glorious Sunday morning outside, and many of the children simply yearned to be running and playing out in the endless fields.

At one end of the church were the heavy, arch-shaped wooden doors that were the only entrance to the vast building. Set along the floor between that and the altar were rows upon rows of pews, brimming with the people of Riverbrook as they listened eagerly to the Service.

And then beyond the altar lay a single door that led to Father Peter's private quarters, for he lived in the church. Beside his quarters were stairs that wound their way up to the spire and the bell tower protruding high into the sky, creating a distinct horizon from afar.

Hundreds of candles, hanging chandeliers, murals of angels and demons alike again, and great stone carved statues, all decorated the inside of the nave, and at least made the enormous space look more filled and purposeful.

Below the enormous, golden chandeliers, of all different shapes and sizes and ages and backgrounds, sat the villagers of Riverbrook that lined the pews. They all looked on eagerly at Father Peter as he spoke, totally absorbed by his powerful voice and by his enormous presence: the only one in the village capable of totally filling such a vast room.

Mostly the audience was made up of families, mothers and fathers with their children, all dressed up in their best frocks and suits for the occasion.

Dotted here and there were couples without children. Some were elderly who had lived their fair share, and were now enjoying their time as grandparents, whilst others were only young couples or newlyweds, perhaps having moved to Riverbrook to start afresh.

Such a thing was not uncommon.

Though nobody had ever really stopped to wonder why, Riverbrook seemed to have that attraction for the young. They often came from far and wide to live here, even if, perhaps, when they originally set off, they didn't know exactly where they were heading.

Johnathan Davies sat with his family of four, almost as central as they could possibly have been in the rows of pews. Though slim and slight, he was a tall boy for his tender age of twelve years, and it was obvious he was going to be tall, broad and strong when he became a man, though of course for now he had none of these qualities.

Johnathan's dark hair and eyes were most striking however, and certainly distinguishable against the rest.

His clothes were plain, but smart, and usually saved exclusively for Services. The young boy wore a white shirt and black trousers, both of which were slightly too big for him, but he would grow into them soon enough.

Johnathan sat beside his father: a tall man with sandy brown hair, much lighter than his son's, and rich blue eyes. His frame, average in height, was not overly broad, but instead it could be described more accurately as wiry.

He had the strength of a regular man, but nothing more.

He wore a suit and tie and black leather shoes, although the shirt was also slightly too big. Unfortunately though, he would never grow into it, for it was made for a broader, taller man.

Nonetheless though, Johnathan looked up to his father and idolised him.

And so a boy should do.

Next along the pew sat Johnathan's mother. Garbed in her best dress, a lovely, rich blue garment that not only accentuated her petite, yet divine figure, but also matched the colour of her eyes.

She was nothing short of beautiful.

A silver chain and small pendant hung about her neck, framed by her long, blonde hair that fell almost haphazardly about her shoulders, though still didn't look scruffy in any way.

Johnathan's parents, Richard and Emily Davies, were well known and liked throughout Riverbrook, and had lived there with their children since Johnathan and Maddie were only babies.

Maddie was younger than Johnathan, though not really by much, and she sat through the Service on the other side of her parents to her brother.

Of only nine years of age, almost ten, she was the definition of adorable. Like her mother, Maddie was very intelligent, even for her age, and she was petite too, again taking after her mother.

And, of course, though her body had not developed in the way her mother's had yet, that would simply be a matter of time.

At the moment her blonde hair and blue eyes were sweet and adorable, but given another ten years they would undoubtedly be stunning and elegant and attractive. Certainly, if she followed in her mother's footsteps at all, which was altogether the most likely outcome, she would most certainly become a little heartbreaker.

At that present moment in time however, such thoughts were as far from Maddie's mind as they possibly could have been, for at that tender age they are by no means a priority.

She leaned forward slightly, stealing a sneaky glance over to her left, past her parents, below their level of eyesight, and pulled a silly face at her brother, as was one of her all-time favourite amusements.

Johnathan smirked in return but tried to act as if he hadn't noticed, partly because he knew his actions were much more obvious that Maddie's, and he was 'supposed to know better', and partly because he knew it drove her crazy.

After a few more moments however, it all became too much, as Maddie stuck her tongue out at him, and he flared his nostrils and widened his eyes in return, forcing her to stifle a giggle.

But it was, unfortunately, exactly at that point that their parents broke their gaze and looked down. A single, stern glance from his father stumped Johnathan's antics, and her mother halted Maddie's silliness just as effectively, though of course it took them both a few minutes of intense concentration to swallow their own laughter.

"Thank you, my friends…" Father Peter finally came to conclude his Service then, and a few scuffles and stirrings amongst the pews began, though out of respect no one yet moved.

Johnathan took the chance to steal yet another glance over at his sister, only to find that her cheeky smirk was already looking his way, forcing him to stifle his laughter once more.

"It's been my pleasure as always, please, enjoy the rest of this splendid day…"

And with that, gesturing openly with his hands and raising his arms slightly, Father Peter released his audience from their captivation, and they immediately broke into courteous applause, though even as they did so they also rose to their feet in swarming droves.

Some, those who seemed in more of a rush, simply smiled thankfully at Father Peter, and he nodded and smiled back understandingly, as they departed almost immediately.

Others though, including Johnathan's mother and father, remained behind to speak with the Vicar personally, and Johnathan watched curiously as Father Peter greeted each and every one of his guests with equal enthusiasm. It seemed to the young boy that this mysterious old man had the most incredible memory, for he knew each person's name in the village, every family's address, and all the troubles they were working through, asking about each in turn and always offering his positive words in reply.

Eventually, a parting in the throngs before them opened and Johnathan's mother and father moved forward to greet Father Peter. Johnathan and Maddie followed dutifully behind, though for some reason as they pressed onward towards the kind, old man, Johnathan felt somewhat apprehensive.

"Thank you for all your help, Father." One man said, shaking the Vicar's hand enthusiastically.

Johnathan recognised him as the owner of the village shop, and rumours had spread some time ago, as they always do, about his wife being unable to bear children. Clearly, and unsurprisingly, Father Peter had been very supportive throughout the matter.

"Not at all, Dorian, not at all." Father Peter replied smiling. "Please give my best to Amanda."

"I will." Dorian responded, nodding as he did so. "Of course, thank you again."

Dorian, the shopkeeper, turned on his heel then and made his way down between the pews, and Father Peter turned to his right to face the Davies family as they approached.

Of course, he smiled when he saw them, but Johnathan couldn't help but notice the generous man's gentle expression change and harden slightly as he laid eyes upon them.

It may simply have been a trick of the candlelight in the enormous room, but as soon as Johnathan considered that possibility, he dismissed it just as quickly.

No.

Something had definitely struck the old Vicar's mind then, and not something good.

Whether it was the first time, or whether Johnathan simply hadn't noticed it before, for it was such a minute and unremarkable change that it was almost impossible to tell, the young boy hadn't a clue.

What he did know, however, was that this time at least, it hadn't simply passed him by, and he noticed Father Peter's change in emotion and character quite obviously.

"Emily...Richard..." Father Peter greeted Johnathan's mother and father expansively, kissing his mother's cheek and grasping his father's hand firmly, though it was painfully obvious that Richard's return handshake was somewhat less robust.

Emily was about Father Peter's height, for he was not overly tall, but then Richard didn't swamp either of them, for his frame was only average.

The old man looked to Maddie and Johnathan then, finding as always Maddie's playful character most charming, but seemingly surprised by Johnathan's wary and inquisitive expression.

"My, how quickly you two are growing! I can barely keep up!" He said regardless, welcoming them

12

with open arms, though his eyes subtly studied Johnathan's expression.

The old Vicar was indeed right, however. Maddie had grown, though she was still not tall for her age, whilst Johnathan, on the other hand, was very tall for only twelve years, and would undoubtedly tower over the lot of them.

Maddie giggled.

Johnathan forced a smile.

Father Peter's eyes flickered between them for a moment, lingering on Johnathan for just a moment too long, before he turned his gaze briefly back to Emily.

But it was then, as his gaze fleeted back to Johnathan's mother, even though it was only for the briefest second, the young boy saw in that moment that they were filled with pain, and something deep inside of the young boy stirred and awakened.

What he saw and what he felt, he did not know. But even just that confusion and unknowing, told Johnathan that whatever it was he saw and felt, wherever it came from, it was a secret.

And for good reason.

"Emily, Richard, I don't suppose you'd mind if I speak to Johnathan for a moment do you, please?" Father Peter asked then. It was less of a request, Johnathan noticed, and more of a statement, but he awaited their responses nonetheless, patiently and courteously.

His mother only smiled though, apparently unaware of what had passed between them, and nodded at Johnathan to tell him it was fine. His father looked perhaps a little more perturbed, but he said nothing of it, and Father Peter did not wait for him to speak up, leading Johnathan over to a newly unoccupied pew, just a dozen or so paces across the room.

Richard glanced at Emily briefly, but she did not return his gaze, and instead looked on almost expectantly after her son.

She then almost immediately took Maddie's hand.

"Come on Maddie." She encouraged her young daughter, for she too was looking inquisitively after her brother. "Let's sit down and wait for Johnathan."

Curious though she may have been, Maddie simply smiled and nodded, following her mother to the opposite side of the nave. They wove through the still talking and laughing crowds and took a seat in the wooden pews there.

Wondering what in the world was so important, and apparently so secret too, Johnathan automatically followed Father Peter to the pews and sat down almost robotically beside him, helpless to the old man's presence.

Nonetheless though, Johnathan was feeling most deductive and inquisitive, for some strange reason, and he kept his wits about him, not wanting to miss even the slightest glance or change in expression.

For a moment then, sat sideways on the narrow bench so as to face the young boy, Father Peter just looked at Johnathan, with a mixture of care and deep concern and worry painted across his face all at the same time. Or at least, as far as the boy could tell.

Young Johnathan was almost coming of that age now where he was no longer a boy, but not quite a man either, and that is always a difficult time, for there is much confusion and disarray. He wasn't even aware of the struggles he was beginning to face, nor of the new awareness of the world all about that was slowly descending upon him, but nonetheless, it was most certainly happening.

And so, as they sat there, in complete silence for a few minutes, each one studying the other in the utmost detail, Emily looked on expectantly from across the room.

Exactly what she was looking for, her husband could not decipher, and Maddie too watched with curiosity and confusion painted across her face. Her mother seemed not in the least bit concerned that Father Peter and Johnathan hadn't yet spoken.

It all seemed most peculiar to little Maddie.

Everyone else gave the pair sat in silence a wide and respectful birth. It was as if they knew that this particular conversation, though it hadn't yet even begun, was the most important of them all in the room at that precise moment in time.

Regardless though, Johnathan ignored all of it, blocking out everything that was happening around him, and simply stared back at Father Peter, trying desperately to decipher what the old man might be thinking.

Eventually Father Peter seemed to relent his search, though Johnathan still had no idea what he'd been looking for, and sat back slightly, exhaling deeply as he did so.

"How are you, Johnathan?" The Vicar asked then, his voice sincere, but at the same time perfectly level, as if the balance of the world hung on Johnathan's reply.

"I'm very well thank you Father." The young boy answered politely. "How are you?"

Father Peter smiled kindly then, though he seemed to be smiling through some kind of adversity that Johnathan simply could not place.

His features finally softened and he spoke again.

"I am very well thank you my boy. And how is school? I've heard that Maddie has moved up into your class? Are you helping to look after your sister?"

By this point, as the Vicar's words reached his ears, Johnathan finally realised that he would not discover the meaning of this conversation today, and eased his searching slightly, though admittedly with faint disappointment.

Curiosity not satisfied is often bitter.

"It's very important, especially now that you're becoming a man…" Father Peter noted.

"Yes Father." Johnathan responded. "I always do my best to care for her. She's very important to me." The young boy's words were years beyond him it seemed, but Father Peter seemed not to notice, and was satisfied with Johnathan's honesty.

"Good, good, very good…" He commented, continuing. "It doesn't matter how old Maddie gets, Johnathan…" The old man mused, leaning in slightly as he spoke. "Even when you are both grown up, and

each have families of your own, you will still always
need to look out for her. You will always need to be
her Knight in shining armour." He explained to the
boy with a whimsical smile dancing across his lips as
he spoke, and his strange choice of words sparked
Johnathan's raging thoughts once again.

Deciding to take the Vicar's words at face
value however, Johnathan smiled and nodded in clear
agreement with the old man, vowing silently to
himself never to let Maddie down.

Nonetheless though, he couldn't help but still
attempt to decipher the real meaning behind Father's
Peter's bizarre comments.

But all too soon it seemed that their strange
conversation came to a swift and somewhat abrupt
end, and Father Peter rose to his feet, gesturing with
his hand for Johnathan to do the same. He guided the
young man back over to where his family sat, on the
opposite side of the aisle in the pews adjacent to
where they'd talked.

They were all looking on at him quite
expectantly, Johnathan thought, especially his mother,
and he felt as though he had somehow not delivered
on some part of an arrangement that he knew nothing
of.

Emily Davies thanked Father Peter for all of
his help, embracing the old man briefly, yet fondly,
and again Johnathan felt something pass between
them, and a sudden wrench in his gut crawled
painfully up and into his chest.

But just as quickly as it had begun, the
horrible feeling passed, and Father Peter bid them all
farewell in turn, thanking them too, and before

Johnathan knew it there was fresh air in his lungs and warm sunshine upon his face.

He felt as though he'd been in the church for not a morning, but instead a decade, and though his senses had been heightened by the whole ordeal, everything seemed to return to normal then, and for the rest of the day he didn't notice anything else out of the ordinary.

The Service had concluded, despite all of the intriguing build up, quite anticlimactically, Johnathan thought. Now everybody was dispersing back to their homes, all scattering off in different directions, and the strange conversation seemed already to be forgotten by all.

Outside the sun was almost blinding, and it took a few minutes for his eyes to adjust to the light.

Maddie bumped into his side and whispered in his ear so that their parents couldn't hear.

"What did Father Peter say?" She hissed.

Johnathan could tell that everyone in the village was equally intrigued, for the inquisitive looks they were all casting in his direction were nothing if not obvious.

"He just asked how school was." He replied with a shrug, but then a smirk crossed his face. "And if I was looking after you." He added.

"What!?" His sister exclaimed then, only just about managing to stifle her voice so that their mother and father, walking just ahead of them, didn't hear. "I'm the one who looks after you!" She hissed playfully again, poking her brother in the ribs. He smiled and put his arm around her shoulder, squeezing her tight.

He was quite a lot taller than Maddie, and her shoulder buried into his ribs, but Johnathan didn't mind, walking home the rest of the way in that embrace.

The day pressed on, as days always do. Especially Sundays, Johnathan thought: he often wondered why the most enjoyable day of the week always had to pass so much more quickly than all the rest.

Fortunately, the sunshine remained strong for the rest of the afternoon, and since the folk of Riverbrook did not work on Sundays, the children of this little rural community very soon found their way to the vast meadows that surrounded the village. Flooded with warmth and golden light and scattered here and there with some thicker and some thinner copses, the huge commons were the perfect setting for enormous games of tig and hide and seek.

These games often lasted for hours on end, and since there was no need to cut them short on days such as this, parents and grandparents wandered the meadows too, enjoying the afternoon in the warmth of the sun and watching their children and grandchildren all run and laugh and play together, enjoying themselves in the way they should.

There were the odd single figures amongst the scattered couples, and a few trios here and there too.

It was something of an unwritten law, an unspoken rule, within this close knit community, that marriage was for life.

That was simply the way it had always been.

And so it should be.

Those that stood alone amidst the crowds, or that had attached themselves temporarily to another couple, simply for the joy of conversation, were all either of bachelor status, or had been widowed through unfortunate circumstances.

For the young, unmarried men and women amongst the scattered crowds, this didn't pose a problem.

As a matter of fact, for them, these were exciting times, for their entire lives of love lay ahead of them.

For those that had been widowed however, through one unfortunate circumstance or another, remarriage was never really an option, for they were still considered bound to the person they had devoted themselves to.

And, needless to say, divorce was a subject never even discussed.

The qualities of trust and respect and faithfulness, lost though they may have been in other places, meant much more to many of the people here than most else.

That was just the way things were.

That was just the way things had to be.

All too soon though, as is always the way, the sun dipped its head down towards the horizon far to the west, and the scattered games and wanderings through the meadows surrounding Riverbrook slowly ceased and dispersed.

Meandering back amongst the thatched, stone cottages, with small wooden, painted doors and low beamed windows, the families each filtered back to their homes as evening fell upon the village that wove its very existence down the banks of the river.

The river didn't cross through the town, for the river had been there long before the buildings had. Instead, it was indeed the town that encroached upon the river's banks, but then, all things considered, the river didn't really seem to mind.

Johnathan and Maddie reluctantly followed their parents back home, of course not wanting to leave the meadows, but knowing that they had school the next morning, they knew they would have to go to bed sooner or later.

They devoured the supper that their mother prepared in what seemed like minutes, consisting of fresh bread and warm tomato soup, for their afternoon of racing around had made them ravenous. Johnathan and Maddie both were still buzzing with energy, excited from their joyous afternoon.

Soon after supper though, with warm food in their bellies and their adrenaline fading, waning, weariness swiftly descended upon the two of them, for of course they were still only young, Johnathan twelve, and Maddie only nine.

Regardless of the fact that they were tired however, Johnathan still nudged Maddie as they turned to head upstairs, under instructions from their father to get ready for bed.

She threw him one of her cheeky smirks in return, her blue eyes glittering mischievously, and Johnathan knew she would try to get him back as soon as they were out of sight of their parents.

It was a game they played constantly. There was never a winner or a loser: it was just fun.

Inevitably, once they had ascended the creaking wooden stairs of their cottage home, Maddie poked her brother in the ribs again, this time aiming instinctively for the spot where she knew he was ticklish and most sensitive. He squirmed away from her and she laughed gleefully and ran to her room.

Johnathan turned immediately to follow, but a scraping chair and a firm voice halted him in his tracks.

"Enough!" Their father called up the stairs. "You had better be ready for bed by the time I get up there!"

It wasn't a threat, of course, and their father's voice wasn't overly authoritative, but both Johnathan and Maddie both knew not to push their luck too far.

Nonetheless, Johnathan's sister still poked her head round her bedroom door one last time and stuck her tongue out at him before waving and disappearing for the night. Johnathan smiled and retired to his own bedroom, yawning deeply as he did so.

He lit a candle by which to see and readied himself for bed. The burning wax threw a dancing orange light across the room, illuminating the single wooden bed pressed up against the one wall. The second wall was lined with a wardrobe and chest of drawers, wooden and chipped here and there, but nonetheless fit for purpose.

Looking across to his left, the third wall framed a single window that by day looked out towards the river in the distance, but for now, with darkness engulfing the village, it showed Johnathan only a dim reflection of himself holding a candle on a tray.

As the young boy threw on his nightclothes then, a set of cotton trousers and a plain buttoned shirt, he caught a glimpse of himself in the mirror that sat on the floor, propped up against the wall on the fourth side of his room, next to the door.

It was quite a large mirror, and Johnathan could see the full length of his body in it. It had at one time belonged to his grandfather, or so his mother had told him at least.

He had never known his grandfather, for he had died before Johnathan was born.

Nevertheless though, he felt a strange attachment to this mirror that the young boy couldn't quite describe, and he had always cherished it.

It was housed in a silver, oval frame that was pristine and perfect, though it must have been very old. Swirling patterns that must have taken many painstaking hours to craft decorated its top and sides and base, and even in the two top corners of the mirror, constructed entirely from silver too, were two birds with their wings spread wide and welcoming, each within its own metallic ring.

It was a lovely thing, and Emily had kept it always for Johnathan.

She had said once that his grandfather would have wanted him to have it. Johnathan had of course asked more about the mirror, for children are nothing if not curious, but when he had done, it seemed to upset his mother for some reason, so he had not asked again.

Instead, the young boy had spent many hours inventing wild and imaginative stories as to exactly how the mirror had come to be. Crazy adventures of heroism and bravery where the brave conqueror had slain a dragon or great beast of some description, and the mirror had been his grand prize.

Johnathan realised then he was still gazing into the reflective face of the mirror, his image dancing orange and yellow in the candlelight. He felt as though he wasn't really looking at himself however, rather that he was looking just into the mirror instead.

That made no sense though, even as the thought crossed Johnathan's mind. After another moment or two, not really knowing exactly what he was looking at anymore, let alone what he was looking for, he shrugged the feeling off and, overcome by a sudden sweeping weariness, descended into bed.

He blew out the candle as he did so, casting the room into sudden darkness, though unknowingly he left the flickering remains of the dancing light cast across the surface of the mirror.

It shimmered even still, reflecting the trembling light across its face, though of course that was impossible.

But it was too dark for Johnathan to see, and so he didn't notice the shapes and figures that the mirror cast in the darkness of that long night, sweeping cross its face in the night, watching him as he slept.

Chapter Two

The following morning, on the whole, was a very normal start to the day for the Davies household, and nothing whatsoever out of the ordinary happened.

Though, evidently, that didn't depict that the rest of the day would follow the same course.

As per usual, Johnathan and Maddie threw each other silly faces over their breakfast of porridge oats, entertaining themselves for the morning as they got ready to go to school.

Emily, their mother, prepared breakfasts and washed up and began the house work that she would spend most of the rest of the day doing.

Their father, Richard, ate with them also, though he ate much more quickly, for he needed to leave early every morning. He worked in the city, and though Johnathan didn't know exactly what his father did, he imagined the work was very important.

He looked up to his father greatly, and the man had always promised Johnathan that one day, when he was old enough, he would take him with him to see the city.

The young boy imagined the whole thing would be very grand indeed.

Just the same as he did every morning, Johnathan's father said goodbye to them and kissed their mother at the door. He took the same horse as he always did, and rode off away from Riverbrook. Sometimes he took a horse and cart if he needed to take much with him, or pick anybody up along the way, but more often than not he went alone, with just a change of clothes for when he arrived at work.

Almost before they knew it then, Maddie and Johnathan were fed, washed, dressed, and saying goodbye to their mother for the day. Their school was but a few minutes' walk from their house, for Riverbrook was really not a big place, and she always waved them off every morning from the doorstep.

Johnathan often thought that there were only just enough children in the village to warrant having a school anyway. There were only two classes; the first class was for the younger children, and the second was for the older children.

Once upon a time, the children in the village had all taken their lessons in the church, for the school had not yet been built. Johnathan vaguely remembered that, though he had been only very young, and in the lower class; the one which, as Father Peter had pointed out the day before, Maddie had recently moved up into his class from.

The Vicar had tutored some of the children himself back then, when there was only one teacher in the village: Miss Falcon, the head of the school, and Johnathan's teacher. She was tall and thin with greyed hair, a sternly lined face, a somewhat sour disposition, and a temperament to match. Her clothes were always plain and spotless and well pressed, she always sat bolt upright, and stood with somehow even more perfect posture than that. She actively encouraged her students to do the same, spending seemingly forever telling them not to slouch, and though her efforts sometimes seemed to be in vain, she never once ceased or relented.

She was, however, regardless of how strict she sometimes appeared to be, a fine teacher, and had taught in the church with Father Peter whilst the school had been under construction.

Though they had probably only spent a small part of their lives in Riverbrook, Johnathan couldn't imagine Father Peter or Miss Falcon to ever have lived anywhere else. They were as much a part of the village as the river or the church or the school were, and without them somehow Riverbrook wouldn't have been the same.

They both made up an integral part of Johnathan's life, and indeed the lives of all the children and families in Riverbrook, whether they appreciated it all of the time or not.

"Good morning Johnathan…Maddie…" Miss Falcon greeted them as they approached the school with one eyebrow raised, ready to jump at any opportunity to correct those that passed her.

It was a relatively small building, much smaller than the church, and was made from a mixture of brick and wood rather than stone. The windows were small and square and close to the ground, and the doors were wooden and narrow and chipped here and there from constant use.

"Morning Miss Falcon." Maddie replied instantly, immediately standing bolt upright. Johnathan too took note of his own posture, but as he opened his mouth to speak, a yawn escaped his grasp instead and Miss Falcon gave him a firm and steady look.

"Indeed it is." Johnathan rolled off his tongue following his yawn, stifling a laugh as best he could.

Their teacher raised her other eyebrow to match the first and clasped her hands together behind her back.

"I do hope you're not going to fall asleep in class today…" Miss Falcon noted. Johnathan immediately shook his head and rushed to reply.

"No, no, of course not Miss Falcon." He stammered. "I just didn't sleep very well, that's all…"

He had indeed been very disturbed during the night, and sleep for some reason had come to him in broken bouts that left him feeling much more drained than rested.

"I see…" His teacher replied, lifting her gaze slightly. "Very well then, inside you go."

They both nodded and hurried past their tall, imposing teacher as quickly as possible.

It wasn't fear that drove Miss Falcon's pupils to respect her, far from it. In fact, exactly what it was seemed to be quite indescribable; it was simply a sometimes chilling air of command that she apparently held complete ownership of, turning her often calm and reserved comments into commands delivered like the loudest cracks of thunder.

The school sat a little ways from, but then also quite close to the southern bank of the river that ran across the northern edge of the village. That was, incidentally, how the village got its name, or so Father Peter had told all the children during Service once upon a time, Johnathan remembered.

Voices in the Mirror

There had once been a weary traveller making his way across the open plains of England, the Vicar had told them in this particular Service, which even now for some reason Johnathan could so clearly envisage.

Some would have said he was a brave adventurer, others knew him as a noble Knight, whilst others would simply have labelled him a wandering vagabond.

For some reason, Johnathan remembered then that Father Peter had looked at him quite deliberately whilst he had been talking, and the young boy recalled that the Vicar's expression had been full of knowing, though at the time that had made no sense to Johnathan, and still didn't if he was honest.

Father Peter had then told them of how the traveller, or Knight, or vagabond, whichever name he had chosen to go by, had eventually come across a river. Knowing not exactly where he was, he decided to follow the river south, for it seemed to be the most sensible and logical choice, since he was from further in the reaches of the north.

Eventually, after several days and nights of travel, he reached the very spot upon which the village would someday be built, and for some reason, nobody quite knows what, he decided to stop searching.

Whatever it was he had been looking for, perhaps he had found it here?

Nobody really knew, even to this day.

He had seen rivers in their beginnings, starting life as bubbling brooks, and over time and distance they grew and widened and aged.

And then he knew what he had to do.

He knew it was time for him to settle.

Following that, as if it were an act of fate even, others were drawn to him and to the place he had decided to cease his endless wanderings. These people that joined him were wanderers and travellers alike, and all united with him in his conquest to construct their new home, still rushing in its very beginnings.

And thus, henceforth, that place upon the river where they decided to create their new lives, became known as Riverbrook.

It was said that one of the wanderers that joined him was a beautiful woman from the south, with deep blue eyes and flowing golden hair, and within a year they were wed and started a family.

Something distracted Johnathan from his daydreaming then and he looked up in a blurry daze.

By now they were sat in class and Miss Falcon was delivering to them what was undoubtedly a riveting English lesson, explaining the subtle differences between nouns and pronouns and verbs and adjectives, or something to that effect, Johnathan guessed.

For some reason, even more than usual, he felt very distracted.

He glanced across the room looking for his sister, for Miss Falcon had, quite rightly, had the foresight to separate them. Scanning his gaze quickly across the tiny pond of twenty or so children, many of them siblings too, it took Johnathan mere seconds to catch Maddie's eye.

She smiled as she saw him looking and pulled a face, sticking her tongue out at him across the classroom, though keeping her silliness discreet so that Miss Falcon didn't see.

The two of them were exceedingly well versed in this game, for they played it on a daily basis, and without a second thought Johnathan checked quickly to see if Miss Falcon was looking, and returned the gesture with an equally ridiculous expression.

And so class continued, though exactly how far they delved into the disorienting depths of the English language Johnathan had no idea, for he spent the vast majority of it either daydreaming when Miss Falcon swept her fierce gaze across the class, or entertaining his younger sister whilst her back was turned.

Later that day, once Miss Falcon's English class had concluded and finished evading young Johnathan's attention, he found himself, as always, spending time during break together with his sister Maddie.

The day was wearing on slowly and though it was warm and the sky was for the most part blue, it was broken here and there in patches by cloud, drifting by above silently and forever undisturbed. A light wind carried them overhead and rustled the trees and the plants and the grass all about, and Johnathan and Maddie sat together upon a small grassy embankment, sprawled out on the floor.

On first glance it looked as though the brother and sister had not a care in the world. However, upon closer inspection, it was clear that their efforts were bent entirely to the task of depicting as many different shapes and animals as they could in the clouds floating along above them.

All about the pair, other siblings did their best to ignore each other, playing with friends their own age, each in their own little groups, as children do, segregating themselves from each other, even unintentionally singling some out, whilst glorifying others.

Such is their fickle nature.

Stood across the other side of the oval of grass that was the school's play area, stood Miss Falcon, forever watchful, overseeing all the children. By her side was Mrs Burrows, Maddie's old teacher from before.

She taught the younger class in the school, and was exactly the opposite of Miss Falcon in every way, shape, and form, to such an extent that Johnathan found it quite amusing.

Mrs Burrows was married, and she was shorter and younger and had a very womanly figure, much more pleasing to the eye than Miss Falcon's, with a heaving bosom and rosy cheeks. Her lips were always raised by a smile and she was very kind natured.

Her softly, softly approach meant that she was in no doubt the favourite teacher out of the two. Though she was quiet, she could certainly test the octaves when she needed to, and all knew not to push her too far.

Everybody has a fuse after all.

Nonetheless though, she had dark hair cut to her shoulders, lovely green eyes, a little girl of her own of only seven years old, and, of course, as you would expect, it was extremely difficult for anybody not to like her.

Suddenly then, casting a quick and instinctive glance down from the clouds above him, Johnathan swept his eyes over a group of boys stood only six feet or so from where he and Maddie were sprawled on the grass. His gaze told him very little, but an instinctive niggle at the back of him mind warned him that trouble was coming.

It is a very useful sixth sense that some fortunate people are able to develop.

Sure enough, within only seconds, drawn from their original conversation by nothing in particular, or perhaps simply by the childish human joy of domination, the boy leading the group jerked his head almost unnoticeably towards Johnathan and Maddie, and they all followed him over.

Johnathan sighed under his breath and clasped his hand gently around Maddie's arm, standing as he did so, drawing her attention to what was about to happen, for she had not yet developed that sixth sense, and she rose quickly to her feet also.

"Playing with girls again Davies?" The boy leading the group immediately jested. It was a childish quip, but Johnathan had expected little else. He'd had trouble from this boy before.

He was at least a few years older than Johnathan, which at that age made an enormous difference.

His name was Brock and he was the son of Riverbrook's metalworker and carpenter. His father was very gifted at his trade and had the strength to work with any material. And so, naturally, Brock too was built broadly and with an intimidating amount of strength and weight, easily almost twice Johnathan's size.

"Yes, Brock." Johnathan replied dismissively. "I'm sitting with my sister." His tone however, though not confrontational in the slightest, only served to infuriate the brute.

"Oh, so you don't mind everybody thinking you're a girl too then?" The bully mocked again, trying to entice a response. His apparently clever remark stirred a few sniggers from his throng in tow, feeding his ego ever further.

He wasn't rewarded however, and Johnathan's clearly indifferent attitude just riled him more.

"No, Brock." Johnathan replied, looking up at the brute stood before him with an expression painted across his young face that vaguely resembled boredom.

Brock was practically a whole foot taller, and at least a foot wider than Johnathan.

Brock had no quick witted reply and he hesitated for a moment. Johnathan seized the opportunity immediately and steered Maddie away, heading for biggest and closest crowd of children he could see.

Brock recovered however, just quickly enough to save face in front of his followers, and threw one final, desperate remark after Johnathan, his power as a bully reduced to rubble without a response.

"Just going to run and hide with your geeky sister are you then!?" He called after them, not even really expecting a reply himself.

But something made Johnathan stop then, and he turned slowly back to face Brock, keeping Maddie behind him, his stance protective.

"What?" He breathed at the brute before him, his gaze levelling.

"Oh, didn't you hear?" Brock teased immediately, knowing in that second he had an opening. "Do you have to hide the nerd in the crowd? That's a shame you know…"

At that point Johnathan felt something welling up inside of him, but he didn't move for a moment, besides slowly clenching and unclenching his fists.

"She's not that bad you have to hide her away you know…" Brock continued, successfully driving Johnathan's rage even deeper.

It was almost as if a blinding veil descended over Johnathan then, covering his vision and his thoughts. He felt in one moment completely in control, and then in the next, as if his body wasn't even his own: as if another presence was engulfing him almost entirely.

"She's not that ugly …I know she's not the best but…"

But Brock didn't even get chance to finish that sentence, for in that moment Johnathan saw nothing but red.

It swept across his vision in an instant like an invisible blindfold, and all of a sudden his movements were no longer his own.

His body lunged forwards for the bully, arms outstretched and fingers clawing for Brock's throat.

Johnathan was barely even half Brock's size, charging forwards with what looked like not a hope in hell. The bully smiled a wicked, victorious grin, and grabbed Johnathan's wrists as he darted forwards, halting him in his tracks. He was all too happy to swat him down with ease and make a fool out of him as he defended his sister, asserting his own dominance.

After all, what else do bullies want?

But in that moment, with that strange veil that had descended upon him, encompassing him, merging with him even, Johnathan had not the strength of a young boy, desperately struggling against a much bigger and older and stronger enemy, but instead he somehow had the strength of a full grown man.

And it was not just the strength of any old man: it was the strength of a man who had lived and learned, who had loved and lost, who had fought to the death, in every sense of the word.

This was the strength of a man who had travelled to every ends of the Earth to find answers, and yet had only found more questions.

He had the strength of a hero, of a fable, of a legend.

Brock surged forward then in response to Johnathan's charge, throwing his entire weight with him, spurred on by the cheers of his expectant and unruly friends, using the term in the loosest possible way.

Maddie piped up and a lump caught in her throat, fearful for her brother, naturally. This had never happened before. Johnathan had always just ignored them in the past.

But the scuffle did not pan out as expected, for either side.

The bully forced Johnathan back, gripping his wrists and hard as he could, but he managed to push the young boy back barely even half a pace.

Maddie's brother braced hard, planting his feet in the ground, his base solid and immovable.

Splaying his arms to the side Johnathan loosed Brock's grip in a single movement, catching him by surprise and knocking him off balance.

Wasting not a second, the young boy struck immediately, with the knowledge and experience seemingly of somebody far beyond his own years. He landed a glancing blow off Brock's cheek, though he had to reach up above his own height to do so.

The shot was not designed to immobilise, only stun, and expose weakness, and it did exactly that.

Instinctively, seemingly not as experienced as Johnathan, though that surely was impossible, the bully raised his hands to protect his face, exposing his chest and abdomen, unprotected.

Johnathan drove his fists up into the bully's unprotected torso, winding him dreadfully. But he didn't simply let him drop then. He felt Brock's weight slump forward as his legs buckled, and he grabbed him by his shirt, wrapping the material round his fists and up into the scruff of the larger boy's neck, taking his weight entirely.

Somehow then, keeping the same grip, the apparently much smaller and younger and weaker boy lifted the bully from his feet, raising him even higher than he already stood, and in the same swift, practiced movement, forced his arms forwards and launched him through the air, sending him flying and sprawling against the base of an oak tree, easily a dozen feet or more away.

The stunned crowd that had gathered around all backed away in fear from Johnathan then, their retracing steps wary and fearful.

Johnathan ignored them though, and just looked on at Brock lay squirming at the base of the tree.

His work was done. His point had been made.

He need do nothing else.

Simply looking on for another moment or two, the young boy went back to slowly clenching and unclenching his fists, calming his rage.

Brock's followers all immediately departed: some friends they were, and Johnathan continued to compose himself.

The haze that had descended over him slowly lifted, and he blinked a few times as if returning to reality.

Maddie rushed to her brother's side and clasped her small hands around his arm.

"Johnathan!" She hissed through clenched teeth, her heart racing and fear and confusion coursing through her veins. She was going to check he was alright, but he beat her to the words.

"Are you ok?" He said immediately.

"Of course!" She replied, as if his question was ridiculous. "Are you ok!?" The shock and panic and upset in her voice was all too clear. She had no idea what had happened. But then, neither did

Johnathan, for he had absolutely no clue what had come over him, and how on Earth he'd been able to do what he'd just done.

But there was no time to wonder, and Johnathan knew it.

"Come on!" He urged suddenly, taking Maddie's hand. "We have to go!"

He knew instinctively, as most children do, that to remain at the scene of trouble is simply begging to be reprimanded.

But he spoke not a moment too soon, for all fell silent in that instant, and an all too stern and familiar voice cut through the air like a knife.

"MASTER DAVIES!"

Chapter Three

Johnathan sat outside Miss Falcon's office, alone in the corridor of the empty school. Since there were only two classes, there were consequently only two classrooms, and they were located at opposite ends of the small building, joined by the single corridor within which Johnathan now sat.

Between them, separating them, was a single, small room which was the school's only office.

Though Miss Falcon and Mrs Burrows shared the office, it had always been referred to as being Miss Falcon's, and Mrs Burrows had never really seemed to mind.

Sat in silence, awaiting what would undoubtedly be his disciplinary fate, Johnathan passed the time by examining the corridor about him in the greatest possible detail he could, and straining his ears to the sounds creeping in from outside.

The corridor was narrow and the walls were built of thick wooden planks, lined horizontally all the way up to the ceiling where the planks cut across above his head. The floor was quite dirty, though it was often cleaned; things are always difficult to keep clean and tidy when there are children around.

The corridor was growing ever darker as the afternoon laboured on and the sunlight faded slowly away. The only windows were at each end of the corridor, next to the doors to each classroom, and occasionally faces would appear at the panes to ogle down the corridor at him.

They would always quickly disappear however, as Mrs Burrows politely shooed the children away, giving Johnathan his privacy back, although she would throw him a quick, sympathetic smile, for she knew perhaps better than anyone, for she saw it used the most often, the sharpness of Miss Falcon's tongue when the matter at hand was a disciplinary one.

Shouts and screams reached Johnathan's ears occasionally and he yearned to be outside with Maddie enjoying the rest of the day. It didn't matter that a barrage of clouds was creeping in overhead. It wouldn't even have mattered once darkness had descended completely. It was simply his sister's company that he enjoyed.

And then, as if she'd had the same thought, Maddie appeared at the dirty window at the far end of the corridor, past Mrs Burrow's classroom, her face darkened and hidden almost completely by shadow as evening encroached, but he knew it was his sister without a flicker of a doubt.

Johnathan turned to her and spread his hands, as if asking what she was doing. She only shook her head in response and pointed at him, raising her eyebrows. He knew she was asking if he was ok, and he just smiled and nodded, shrugging his shoulders as if to say he didn't know what was going to happen.

Their parents, Richard and Emily Davies, were in the office with Miss Falcon, undoubtedly deciding what was to be Johnathan's immediate fate. Maddie was supposedly under the watchful eye of Mrs Burrows, but then so were all the other children, until they either left to return home, or until their parents arrived to collect them.

Miss Falcon had made a special point of sending for Johnathan's parents following the incident earlier.

Maddie disappeared suddenly then as if she had been wrenched away from the window against her will, though of course that wasn't the case, and Mrs Burrows appeared yet again. Her face was filled with a sorrowful expectancy, though her expression now was laced slightly with contemplating thought, for no one who had seen what Johnathan had done knew exactly quite how he'd managed it.

If he strained his hearing he could just about make out the muffled voices of Miss Falcon and his mother and father through the thick wooden door to the office. He couldn't distinguish what they were saying however, only who was speaking at any given time.

His heart leapt from his chest, feeling as though it would come flying out of his mouth, every time he heard a chair leg scrape on the cold, stone floor within. But, as of yet, he had received no scalding.

The light crawling in through the two windows at each end of the corridor dimmed yet again, though Johnathan could still faintly see the trees outside through the murky glass. Their leaves and branches whipped about carelessly, and it seemed as though the wind had picked up considerably as night encroached.

He shivered, not so much from cold, though the day was most certainly heading that way; perhaps somebody had stepped on his grave.

Suddenly then the mumbling voices ceased and all three chairs scraped on the floor simultaneously.

This was it.

The young boy did his best to swallow his nerves.

The cane perhaps? Johnathan thought to himself. That was usually Miss Falcon's preferred punishment.

It was quick and easy and got the point across.

Solitude maybe? He thought then.

Perhaps not, he reconsidered. It took too long and required too much of her time to keep checking on him.

More than likely both, he decided, all things considered.

He imagined she wouldn't mind making the effort.

It could be much worse, he conceded silently, indeed before judgement had even been passed.

But then, at the same moment as the door handle to the office turned and squeaked, swinging the door slowly and menacingly open, the door at the far end of the corridor clicked open too, next to the window where Maddie had only just been, and opposite Mrs Burrow's classroom.

In strode Father Peter, his small figure looming into the corridor, just as Miss Falcon appeared at Johnathan's side, with his parents close behind.

Miss Falcon's gaze was steady and hard and cold, but Father Peter's expression, just about visible in the dim light, and even his pace and stride, were not only meaningful, but even purposeful.

His forehead was creased with concern: the type of worry that comes about when a man knows more than he wished he did, and his eyes pooled with worry.

Though the Vicar's lips were stiff and taught with determination, it was not his intent to punish, quite clearly, but instead to remedy.

Johnathan looked up briefly to his parents too, and their faces were relatively grim, and his mother, Emily, glanced down at him with equal worry, but admittedly also confusion in her eyes.

"Father Peter." Miss Falcon greeted the old man sharply, nodding her head briefly in acknowledgement, though rather curtly, Johnathan noted. The feigned surprise in her tone however did not go unnoticed, and it was all too obvious that she thought this was none of the Vicar's business.

She stood somehow even taller and even straighter than she usually did, towering over the short man approaching her, asserting her dominance with full force, unwilling to back down even in the slightest.

However, the second Father Peter locked his eyes with hers, opening his mouth calmly and assuredly to speak, her defences crumbled, and his overwhelming aura consumed all. His presence was by no means malicious, but it was so overpowering that Johnathan could literally feel it seeping along the corridor, and he saw Miss Falcon falter terribly beneath it.

"Amanda…" Father Peter hailed her in return, speaking that single word as if he had just recited volumes.

Johnathan had never heard anybody call Miss Falcon by her first name before, and it threw her even more.

He said nothing else for a moment or two, but simply bore his calm, easy gaze into Johnathan's uptight teacher. She stared back, her eyes flinty and her expression cold, but behind her tough façade, even the young boy could see her fading, and fading fast at that.

"What can I do for you, Father?" She finally asked, though she spoke almost completely through gritted teeth.

"I've heard about the commotion this afternoon…" He replied coolly, glancing around casually. "I've come to offer assistance, if I can…"

"With all due respect Father…" Miss Falcon began, though Johnathan could sense the rigid bitterness in her words. "We are perfectly capable of dealing with this ourselves."

Her response was blunt, surprisingly so, but Father Peter seemed not in the slightest perturbed.

"Troublemakers must be disciplined." She continued.

"Oh, of course." Father Peter agreed immediately. "You are right, naturally. This decision lies solely in your hands." His words were for Miss Falcon, but as he spoke he looked round and Emily and Richard also, his expression entirely unreadable.

"I see…" Miss Falcon replied, more to have something to say than for any other reason.

"But there is always a good lesson to be learned from these little mishaps. I simply want to make sure that, whatever you decide to be a fitting punishment, young Master Davies not only receives it, but indeed also learns the lessons he needs to learn from this little misfortune."

It was at that moment that Johnathan first witnessed and appreciated the full extent of the power that Father Peter commanded.

His voice was the immutable word of the Church: words that everyone respected and feared so.

Johnathan saw Miss Falcon's eyes flash, but in the momentary silence that followed, Johnathan felt the old man's power surge silently and undetectably through the corridor, washing over the four of them in his presence, engulfing them entirely. Next, he felt Miss Falcon's will smoulder and sizzle and shatter and break, all almost in the same instant.

She sighed deeply, somehow exhaling all the pent up wrath and aggravation that had so clearly been meant for him.

Johnathan shuddered slightly at the thought.

That single breath signified her defeat, and Miss Falcon's posture and position faltered also, for the first time that Johnathan had ever seen.

"Very well Father…" She conceded. "I believe Master Davies was only standing up for himself, and for his sister, Maddie, though he was perhaps a little too heavy handed for my liking…"

Her words came with a stern look for Johnathan, but if that was as far as his punishment from her was going to extend to, and it certainly looked that way after Father Peter's intervention, the young boy could most definitely live with it.

Though, of course, he was not stupid, and he managed to keep himself from smiling. Instead he wore a very stern, very serious, and utterly ashamed expression of guilt, making it as convincing as he possibly could.

Miss Falcon seemed to buy it, for after a moment she looked back to Father Peter, apparently challenging his calm, piercing gaze one last time. After but a few seconds however, wavering yet again under his relaxed composure, she soon looked away once more, and in that moment it was over.

Father Peter nodded, almost imperceptibly, though Johnathan saw it, and Miss Falcon dropped her gaze entirely.

His father opened his hand then in the smallest of movements, but Johnathan recognised it as a disappointed beckoning, and rose immediately to his feet.

"Actually, just a moment please Richard…" Father Peter spoke again then, raising his hand slightly and seeming to freeze them all in place with that simple gesture, though of course that wasn't true in the slightest.

It couldn't have been.

It was simply his presence and his aura that always held his audience so captivated, surely.

Richard faltered too for a moment, opening his mouth to speak, but not knowing what to say. He stammered for a second before ceasing his efforts completely.

"I would like to speak with the boy, with your permission of course." The old Vicar requested politely, though, again, while his words were calm and soft and not authoritative in the slightest, his meaning was undoubtedly final.

It was not actually a request, in any sense of the words, really. He wasn't asking them for permission, he was courteously telling them what was going to happen.

Johnathan's father even thought about denying Father Peter his request, for the most meagre of moments, before his will also crumbled and his gaze dropped just as submissively as Miss Falcon's had done.

The silence that followed then translated quite plainly as:

'I am going to speak with Johnathan, and I will return him home whenever I am finished.'

Though no words were spoken, that was exactly what was said, and all knew it.

Richard's gaze still remained low, as did Miss Falcon's, both of them defeated and submissive, overwhelmed entirely it seemed.

Johnathan's mother however, Emily, did not seemed phased in the slightest, and when she looked into Father Peter's eyes, her expression was not one of challenge like her husband's or Miss Falcon's had been, but something else entirely.

The young boy struggled to find the words to describe it. Perhaps the only words he could find to match the look in his mother's eyes was one that made not really much sense at all.

She looked hopeful.

Yes, there was most definitely hope in her gaze, but the more Johnathan looked on as they held each other's attention for a second or two longer, the more he saw something else entirely. It was something that had grown within her now for so long that it was so obviously, and then also somehow at the same time so imperceptibly, bursting at her seams.

Desperation.

Yes, that's what it was. Johnathan recognised it somehow, and the look in his mother's eyes tore at the young boy's heart. And Father Peter knew it, for the look in his own eyes was understanding and caring as he gazed upon poor Emily.

She looked fraught, despairing, lost.

Father Peter opened his hand then, and Johnathan rose obediently to his feet, and without another word followed the old Vicar as he nodded his head to his audience, releasing them from his grasp.

He turned on his heel and led Johnathan back down the corridor and out into the early evening air, letting the door swing shut with a loud bang behind them, signalling that his word, indeed, was final.

Chapter Four

As they walked, the ground beneath their feet was still vaguely warm, and though the sky was darkening and a barrage of clouds was piling in above, they trapped the heat of the day close to the ground, keeping the air tepid all around.

The wind seemed to have died completely however. The trees and leaves and branches that had stirred so violently earlier now stood completely still.

An eerie silence had fallen over the village, as if a stifling blanket had been laid upon Riverbrook, and all around hovered an air of expectancy.

Johnathan continued to follow Father Peter as he strode casually, though somehow at the same time with overriding purpose, towards the church.

Of course a flurry of questions raced through Johnathan's mind.

Why had Father Peter spared him his punishment?

What was so important that he needed to speak to him now?

Why had he been there in the first place?

How had he known?

He imagined, or hoped at least, that he would get his answers soon enough.

The thing that unnerved Johnathan the most however, was not the peculiar silence, or the encroaching darkness, or even the strangeness of what had come over him that afternoon, which he still had no idea about. It was, in fact, the gawping eyes and gaping mouths of everybody they passed on their short journey to the church.

Everywhere he looked somebody was peering out of a window, or peeking through a doorway, adults and children alike, some pretending to do or look at something else, whilst others simply stared.

It seemed the whole of Riverbrook was afire with curiosity, for news of what had happened had clearly spread fast, as news always does in such a small community.

Finally, after what felt like a lifetime, though was really only five or ten short minutes, they eventually reached the heavy wooden doors that were the entrance to Father Peter's church.

It was almost totally dark now and even the remaining warmth of the day was diminishing.

Father Peter turned the heavy, hanging metal ring that was the door handle and the door heaved open with a groan that made it sound like a great effort. Johnathan followed the old man inside and they closed the door carefully behind them.

The huge room that was the inside of the church, reaching high up into the sky, was almost pitch black, and Johnathan simply stood for a moment, feeling blind and helpless in the vast, overwhelming darkness.

But the Vicar's hands were immediately busy with well-practiced purpose, and within only seconds he had struck a match and set about lighting candles dotted in various places about the church. There were candles on mantles, in great spiralling metal stands, set upon shelves and trays, and he even reached up to the chandeliers above with a long pole, lighting one end of it, and set those burning too.

He beckoned Johnathan to sit while he worked, and the young boy settled in one of the pews towards the front of the hall, closest to the altar. He watched as the old man worked his way methodically around the hall, lighting what felt like hundreds of candles in the process.

Johnathan did however notice that the Vicar missed out many of them, lighting perhaps not even half, for it was unlikely that anyone else would come by this late, and already there was plenty of light to see by.

Eventually Father Peter ceased his frantic workings and walked over to the pew in which Johnathan sat, taking a seat beside him and facing him quite directly, much like he had done after the previous day's Service.

And again, exactly as he had done before, he did not speak immediately, but instead spent a few minutes looking long and hard at the young boy, with the same piercing and inquisitive expression as the other day.

Finally though, for this time Johnathan did not know what to look for in Father's Peter expression, and so he was simply waiting for the Vicar to speak, the old man relented.

"Johnathan…" Was all he said at first, seeming to be unsure of exactly where to start.

"Good evening Father Peter…" Johnathan responded, equally unsure how to reply. "How can I help?"

Father Peter smiled then, though worry crossed his face too, Johnathan noticed.

"I heard about what happened at school…" The old man said then, though Johnathan knew that of course, so again the young boy knew not how to respond.

"It wasn't my fault…" Johnathan eventually started, breaking the momentary silence that had fallen over the vast room.

"I know, Johnathan, I know…" Father Peter reassured him. "I don't yet understand, but I do know…"

The young boy nodded in reply, though in truth he didn't exactly know what the Vicar meant.

He seemed to change tact then, however, and asked Johnathan another question, seemingly out of the blue.

"Why do you come to church, Johnathan?" He inquired.

Johnathan was confused for a moment, not knowing really what answer the old man was looking for.

"Why do I come?" He said, puzzled.

"Yes. Why do you come to the Services? Why attend the Sermons? What does it mean to you?"

Johnathan thought again for a moment, though it was only the simplest of answers that came to the forefront of his mind.

"Because my mother and father bring me." He replied with a slight shrug, as if that was all the reason in the world he needed.

"I see…" Father Peter replied tentatively, thinking for a moment also before speaking again. "Perhaps I was wrong…" He mused.

Contemplation creased Johnathan's forehead again then as he plunged instinctively slightly deeper into thought.

"My mother once told me…" He eventually began, drawing the thought up deep from his memory. "That people come to church because God helps them face their demons. Is that true?"

"She said that, did she?" Father Peter mused for a moment. "Yes, I suppose that would make sense…" He muttered, though Johnathan didn't really think the Vicar was talking to him, and since what he was saying didn't really make sense, the young boy waited patiently for an answer.

Father Peter sighed deeply then and looked directly at Johnathan, his piercingly calm gaze drawing the young boy's whole attention.

"Yes." He said simply then. "Some people come to church because they need help facing their demons."

"Does everybody have demons?" Johnathan asked then, leaning in, captivated all of a sudden, though he wasn't quite sure why he was fascinated so.

"Yes, everybody has demons, Johnathan." The Vicar replied carefully, very interested now too.

"Then why do some people come to church, and some don't?"

It was a perfectly reasonable question.

"Not everyone wants to face their demons, Johnathan." The old man replied, his words filled with calm and accepting truth. "Anyone can choose to come here or not…" Father Peter continued. "But whether they come here to face their demons, or choose to face them alone, it doesn't make a difference. As long as they do it, one way or another, that's all that really matters."

The Vicar's response seemed to stir something deep within Johnathan, and he sat waist deep in thought for a few minutes, turning the old man's words over and over again in his mind, contemplating each and every one.

Finally something seemed to interrupt his trail of thought and he looked up again.

"You said everybody has demons…" He started, and Father Peter nodded. "What are your demons, Father?"

Father Peter smiled as he replied, recognising a question bordering on truth when he heard one.

"I have lots of different demons, Johnathan. They probably wouldn't mean very much to anybody else, but to me, they all mean lots of different things."

"But you've never done anything wrong?" Johnathan questioned then, confused.

The old man laughed suddenly and the sound was rich and deep and filled the vast, empty room.

"Of course I have!" He exclaimed, still laughing lightly. "We're all human Johnathan. We all make mistakes. We have to, or we would never learn…"

Johnathan thought that over for a moment too, and Father Peter could see that something was clearly bothering the young boy, whether he even realised it or not. He had come to some sort of crossroads, and a very important one by the looks of it.

"So what are my demons?" Johnathan eventually asked, and Father Peter's eyes narrowed with both worry and curiosity.

He levelled his gaze at the young man sat before him and looked at him very seriously, attempting in vain to read the expression upon his face.

Eventually, his scrutiny all but unsuccessful, the old man replied warily.

"That's for you to decide, Johnathan. Our demons are our own. I can't tell you what you fear or what you choose or what you regret."

Johnathan's face looked almost set in stone as Father Peter's words washed over him.

"Only you can decide those things." He continued. "And your decision will, in turn, decide what kind of man you grow up to be."

The young boy nodded very seriously in reply, gravely even, as the weight of the Vicar's words sank into his mind.

That was enough now, Father Peter saw quite clearly.

He hadn't heard exactly what he'd expected from the young boy, but in fact, he'd learned much more.

It gave him plenty to think on at least.

Rising slowly to his feet, the old man motioned for Johnathan to do the same. Looking up briefly, gazing about in the flickering candlelight, Father Peter looked about the stained glass windows set high in the walls for a moment, darkened by the black of the night, wondering exactly what on Earth he was supposed to do about all this.

Should he even do anything?

He didn't know.

He felt strangely lost amidst everything that was happening, and whatever was going on, it had certainly only just begun.

He hadn't felt this lost since Emily had come to him all those years ago, in pieces, broken.

And even now, after all this time, he could sense things heading that way once again. They were not only heading that way, but snowballing in fact, gaining speed and momentum unstoppably, and he felt entirely powerless to do anything about it.

The old man looked down at Johnathan for a moment with regret and sorrow painted across his face.

Johnathan looked back, but seemed not to contemplate the danger at hand.

'How could he know?' Father Peter thought to himself. 'He's caught up right in the middle of this, and he doesn't even realise…'

"Come, Johnathan." The anxious Vicar beckoned then. "It's late. Let's get you home."

As if on cue Johnathan yawned a great yawn, feeling drained from his long, eventful day, and nodded eagerly.

By the time Father Peter had led the young boy home however, under the protective cover of darkness, he was no longer keen to get there, for a great weariness had come over him, and he was practically falling asleep as he walked.

Although, Johnathan did briefly realise at one point, that he and Father Peter had barely spoken about the incident with Brock at all, and in fact the whole event seemed to be forgotten, as if lost in the past of so long ago.

He was simply too tired to properly process that epiphany however, and just trudged on towards home, following the strange old man through the darkness.

He was vaguely aware that Father Peter spoke with his parents when they finally reached the house, though he hadn't the energy to listen to what they were saying, since he practically crawled through the front door.

Eventually, Richard relented and carried the young boy up to his bedroom, depositing him gently in bed, where he immediately fell to sleep.

Both of them were unaware at this point however, that in Richard and Johnathan's absence, Father Peter was speaking hurriedly and in a hushed whisper to Emily, Johnathan's mother, and, in a most uncharacteristic manner, his voice shook with fear and anxiety.

Her face paled at his words, though her eyes betrayed confusion also, for what he told her were words she never thought she would hear again.

Chapter Five

For the next few days, in fact, for the next week or so, everything seemed to return to normal, and the world continued to turn just as it had always done. Time passed by uncaring of the trivial pursuits and problems that mankind has an arbitrary and most annoying habit of chasing and following.

Mother Nature doesn't often turn a blind eye to the petty squabbles of men, instead, She makes absolutely certain to ignore them completely. Were it to be any other way, chaos would undoubtedly ensue.

To place that burden upon herself would be madness.

Other people however, seem to be unable to help themselves.

Self-induced pressure causes carnage.

Maddie and Johnathan walked together beneath the bright blue morning sky, cold and clear and exposed.

Their breath steamed in rolling billows as it hit the cold morning air engulfing them. Johnathan walked slowly and scuffed his feet on the ground, though his body was tense, feeling eyes upon him even before they were so.

His younger sister walked close at his side, not quite touching him, but so near she was almost clinging to his arm as they passed by their neighbour's stone cottages, topped with thatch and bindings. It wasn't exactly fear that kept little Maddie so close, but whatever it was wasn't wholly dissimilar.

Sure enough, within minutes, they saw others also filtering out from between the cottages and meandering their way towards the school. They clumped together into small groups, as if for protection, and eyed Johnathan warily, uncertainty in their eyes.

He glanced between them briefly, though he didn't look at them as much as he looked through them, for their behaviour not only distanced them from him, but distanced him from them, if there were even a notable difference.

"Is it going to be like this forever now?" Maddie's voice piped up amidst the morning, reaching Johnathan's ears with a tone slightly quivering.

"No, don't worry…" Johnathan replied, as reassuringly as he could, placing his arm gently around his little sister's shoulders. She wrapped her arms around his body and buried her head against him.

At that moment, Johnathan felt as if comforting Maddie was the most important thing in the world. As if safeguarding her happiness and assuredness was his sole purpose. It was the kind of feeling he would have expected if he ever had children of his own, the young boy thought, in a most bizarre and adult like manner.

Then the pair of them spied Brock in the distance, as the school slowly came into view. Maddie swallowed nervously when she saw him, surrounded as always, but now more than ever, by a gaggle of his followers.

It had been almost a week since the incident, and he had only been back a day or two, having received three broken ribs and a broken arm at the hands of her brother.

Regardless though, it seemed that yet even still nobody was any the wiser as to how exactly Johnathan had managed to manhandle Brock so. The matter remained a mystery, and Maddie clung yet even more tightly to her brother, knowing without a shadow of a doubt that whatever had happened, he had only been protecting her.

The day passed slowly and anxiously, in much the same way as the days preceding it had done. Lessons were unusually quiet, except for the urgent whisperings rippling rumours.

Children will be children.

Nonetheless, all eyes were upon Johnathan seemingly constantly, and all the while his thoughts were of his little sister. For though he didn't care what the others thought or said, he knew the whole matter was upsetting her greatly, and he counted the seconds until every break whereupon she would instantly run to him, fighting back tears.

Miss Falcon loomed ominously it seemed at every turn, ready to launch herself at Johnathan the instant he started to cause trouble.

On the contrary though, he and his sister sat in solitude amidst all the other children. It was almost as if someone had placed an invisible barrier around them, forcing all to steer clear, for there was a void twelve feet across that encircled the pair of them, seemingly everywhere they went.

The day's end couldn't arrive soon enough, and the second that school was dismissed, Maddie and Johnathan were so swift out of the door that the words had barely even left their teacher's lips.

Miss Falcon's steady gaze would follow them out of the door with a mixture of suspicious, confusion, and even slight sympathy pooling behind it.

The journey home was a blur, for they ran the entirety of it, bustling in the front door and racing immediately upstairs.

Had they not been in such a terrible rush, they perhaps would have noticed how eerily quiet the house was.

Usually their mother was busy with housework or cooking or some other task. But on this day, she had found nothing to keep her occupied, or at the very least, nothing that could keep her mind occupied, and instead pulled her bedroom door quietly to when she heard her two children return home, wiping the tears from her cheeks as she did so.

She silently closed it and held her breath, doing the best she possibly could to swallow her sobs and hold back more tears, for the last thing she wanted was for her children to see her like this.

As it was though, they had no idea, for they too had worries and upsets that they did not wish to share, and the house remained silent for many more hours that day.

It was late into the night, far later than he would have liked to have been awake, that Johnathan sat cross legged upon the floor, elbows on his knees and chin resting on his hands, staring at his reflection in the mirror, dancing and shimmering by candlelight.

Of course he had not been able to sleep.

How could he?

It was not the rumours or the unrest amongst his peers that was keeping him awake. As much as those things may bother most people, they were of no consequence to him. The thing that plagued the young boy on this night, and indeed had done for those preceding it too, was that even he still didn't know what had happened.

Somehow he had overcome Brock, which in of itself wasn't the problem, but rather, the fact that he hadn't a clue what had come over him, nor where that inhuman strength that he'd felt had come from, burned more and more questions into his mind.

His expression reflected back at him and did little to ease his worry, for it too was filled with concern and confusion.

As the firelight by which the young boy could see danced to and fro, he caught glimpses of himself in a hundred different lights, and sometimes even it seemed as though the person staring back at him wasn't even him.

The face he studied in his reflection was indeed very similar to his. This face had dark eyes and hair, just the same as Johnathan's, and his features were much the same shape, its chin well defined and cheek bones high.

But, on the contrary, it carried none of the innocence of the twelve-year-old boy sitting before it, and its features were rugged, ravaged by time, and its eyes were hardened, barraged by God only knows what.

Johnathan sighed deeply, wondering in the near blackness who this stranger was he could see in his reflection, so different and yet so similar to himself all at once.

He was far too tired, far too distracted and far too young to realise the insanity of what he was seeing. Yielding to confusion and uncertainty he decided to succumb to sleep.

Clambering to his feet laboriously and blowing out the candle by which he could see, Johnathan crawled into bed and curled up into a ball in the darkness.

Waiting still in the reflection of the the mirror, the figure Johnathan had seen rose to its full height, its body broad and tall and strong. The expression upon its face now was curious, watching Johnathan as he slept.

It pursed its lips for a second, a look of sorrow and regret crossing its face, restricted and frustrated.

The next day followed much the same pattern as the previous. Maddie and Johnathan tore home as the afternoon wore on into evening, and once again the house was eerily silent.

His sister didn't notice once again, and she raced straight away up the wooden staircase. Johnathan went to follow, but this time, for some reason, he picked up on the fact that something wasn't quite right, and paused for a moment.

He stepped cautiously into the kitchen, and then in turn the living room, scanning around for his mother.

She was nowhere to be seen.

He took to the stairs. They creaked warning sirens under his weight as he climbed and he only caught the last moment of movement as his parents' bedroom door closed as he approached the landing.

The young boy of only twelve years thought little of what he had seen, for in all honesty, he had seen nothing. However, for some reason, he thought of what the figure he had seen in the mirror last night would think, and he knew the familiar stranger would sense that something was wrong.

And so, in turn, Johnathan knew without a shadow of a doubt that there was indeed something amiss.

He approached his parents' bedroom slowly and carefully, his movements cautious and wary. Maddie poked her head out onto the landing, wondering why her brother hadn't immediately followed her upstairs. He motioned for her to go back into her room.

She looked confused, but did as he asked.

Somehow knowing that whatever lay beyond the door, it was not for his sister to see, Johnathan wanted to protect her from it, even as he reached out for the door handle. He froze for a second then, straining his ears as he heard light footsteps from within. Changing his mind, opting for a different tact, he curled his hand into a fist and knocked quietly upon the wooden barricade before him.

For a moment nothing changed, and he wondered if he hadn't knocked loud enough. But then, sure enough, the sounds of clunking floorboards gave away movement, and within a moment or two his mother, Emily, opened the door.

"Yes dear?" She asked of her young son, smiling comfortingly at him.

Relief washed over Johnathan then, seeing that everything was alright after all. But once again his thoughts turned to the figure he had seen the night before, and that same strange perceptiveness oozed through the young boy.

Suddenly then all at once he saw through his mother's façade.

Her hands were trembling, only ever so slightly, but still nonetheless it was clear as day. Her cheeks were flushed and her eyes were puffy and red. She was holding back, and Johnathan felt a horrible wrenching in his chest that cut him so deeply it was all he could do to simply stay standing.

A yearning to reach out and hold his mother overwhelmed him, and his muscles locked and stiffened in a fierce battle between uncountable involuntary movements.

"Are you ok, Johnathan?" Emily asked him again, concern crossing her face.

"Yes." He replied quickly. Too quickly in fact, and of course she knew that something was wrong, but he continued. "I just didn't know where you were…"

"Ok…" She replied carefully, her brow furrowing.

The look she saw in her son's eyes was one that she hadn't seen for years, and unknowingly it forced a yearning in her chest that had never really left her.

"How was school?" She asked then, disguising her upset as best she could. "Where's Maddie?"

"I'm here." Maddie piped up then, having heard the brief and concealed conversation from her room.

"How was your day sweetheart?" Her mother asked her with a smile. Maddie approached with a smile, though the question silenced her, and she didn't notice that something was so very wrong, Johnathan observed.

"It was okay…" Maddie lied, badly, dropping her gaze.

Their mother smiled understandingly, her eyes compassionate, for she knew things were difficult at the moment, most certainly, for them all.

"Why don't you take Maddie down the road to see Mister Riley?" Emily suggested to Johnathan then, and immediately Maddie's eyes brightened.

Mister Riley owned a small sweetshop in the centre of the village, right on the banks of the river. He was a kind, humble old man, and one of the very few adults who seemed not in the least bit phased by the occurrences of late.

Plus, he made the best sweets.

Maddie nodded eagerly and Johnathan sighed inwardly and ruefully agreed. He knew that his mother was only getting rid of them so she could compose herself. Undoubtedly, when they returned she would be downstairs concentrating on the housework and cooking dinner, distracting herself from whatever was wrong so that it did not show quite so obviously.

There was, however, very little Johnathan could do about the matter, and he and Maddie departed immediately to visit Mister Riley, a few pennies from their mother in each hand for sweets of their choice.

Sure enough, an hour or so later, as darkness encroached over Riverbrook, Maddie and Johnathan returned home, entering the house to the sound of their mother humming to herself, cleaning, whilst dinner was on the boil.

Johnathan had been spot on with his prediction, it seemed.

He swept through into the kitchen, his eyes everywhere. The pot boiling on the stove whistled in tune with Emily's humming, and his mother's clothes were dirtied from where she had been distracting herself by cleaning.

"Ah, Johnathan, sweetheart." She greeted him with a wide smile. "Lay the table for me please dear." She requested sweetly. "I'm going to go and clean up." She said absently then. "Your father will be back soon…"

He obediently went to the drawer next to the stove and pulled out four sets of cutlery, paced over to the large wooden table, rectangular and chipped here and there, and began to lay out their usual places.

Voices in the Mirror

Emily disappeared upstairs to change and Johnathan listened to the sound of her creaking footsteps as she disappeared up the stairway.

Suddenly, pain wrenched at his heart then and he felt as if someone had punched him in the chest. He clutched at his small torso with his hand, as if somehow that would make the wrenching agony subside, and gasped desperately for air.

After a few seconds the pain was replaced with terrible worry and a chasm opened up in his stomach, as if the pit of it had just collapsed.

He raced upstairs on swift and silent feet, unheard by all, though his movements felt as though they were not his own.

His parents' bedroom door was ajar just half an inch, and he could see the quivering shadows of movement pass over the crack between the door and the frame every few seconds.

He would never normally have done what he did then, for he knew it was most certainly not the decent thing to do. But then, in that moment, he wasn't thinking as his twelve-year-old self, where the world was black and white, he was thinking almost entirely as somebody else, and everything seemed to be a blurry, confusing shade of grey.

In that moment the veil descended over him again, exactly like had happened when he had faced up to Brock, and suddenly, not only his movements, but his thoughts too, were not his own. He felt a burning desire to enter his parent's room and reach out and place his hand upon his mother's shoulder.

But somehow he couldn't move.

He was so confused.

What was happening?

Instead, whatever it was that was restraining him, controlling him, forced him to place one eye up to the crack in the doorway and peek through, and what he saw took his breath away completely.

He saw his mother, dear Emily, of course, as he expected. She was getting changed, ready for when her husband, Richard, returned home.

But when she reached up to adorn a plain, white blouse, pulling it over her head, Johnathan's eyes settled upon her exposed body. Her ribs and back were a dreadful mix of black and blue and purple, bruised and swollen terribly, battered and beaten awfully.

Her wounds were extensive, and some looked a week or more old, while others were fresh as a new day.

Anger welled up inside of Johnathan then, an anger that didn't even feel like his own. But nonetheless, it built within his body, and a sudden desire to find Richard and to kill him, to make him pay for what he'd done, to beat him to death, for everything that he'd done over the long years gone by, almost overwhelmed him entirely.

Johnathan's body was tense and rigid, bristling with fury.

Suddenly then the front door opened sharply and slammed shut again, signalling that Richard was home from work, though he did not call up to greet them.

Still staring through the crack in the doorway, Johnathan saw Emily shudder and sigh deeply, holding her hands trembling to her lips.

Beside himself completely by then, Johnathan turned on his heel towards the stairs and clenched and unclenched his hands purposefully, ready beyond all belief to dispense his decade old wrath.

But then Maddie was there, appearing from nowhere, blocking his path, her eyes fraught with worry and recognition. She saw immediately that Johnathan had been overwhelmed once again.

She still didn't understand it, just as he didn't. She only knew that her dear brother needed her.

Sensing that he wasn't in control, Maddie reached out a trembling hand to her brother and placed it gently on his shoulder. She smiled lovingly, and softly brought Johnathan into a kind embrace. He held her back tightly, and the relief that washed over him in that moment was unrivalled, as if he hadn't been able to hold young Maddie for countless years on end.

He saw her fear.

She was terrified for him and for what he would do, and the veil slowly lifted from his gaze, and his head gradually cleared.

Of course Johnathan didn't want to frighten her, neither he, nor the figure from the mirror, he imagined.

And so, he simply held his sister close, knowing, or at the very least hoping, that everything would be alright.

Chapter Six

Richard was in a foul mood that night. And when the three of them descended to the kitchen to greet him and to serve up dinner as a family, he didn't speak to his wife or children as they sat and began to eat, and barely even looked up from his food.

Johnathan's expression could only be described as thunderous, though he held himself back with fortitude he didn't know he had. His mother, Emily, moved sheepishly and with what seemed to be great fear. It was almost as if she knew what was going on, and even though she was powerless to stop it, somehow she thought that she only had to endure it a while longer, and the terror would eventually pass.

Maddie sensed that something was terribly wrong, but, as of yet, had no idea what it was.

After what felt like many long, slow hours, the meal finally ended. Johnathan and Maddie and their mother took the dishes and washed and dried them, and Richard, without so much as a word, retired for the night.

More than once Emily splayed her hands upon the table and leant forward heavily onto her arms, seemingly supporting her exhausted and beaten frame, just desperately trying to keep herself upright. Maddie didn't really notice, but Johnathan most certainly did, and his heart was in his mouth when they eventually finished and turned in for the night themselves.

He watched his mother close her bedroom door with a shaking hand.

Johnathan sat with Maddie silently in the darkness until she fell into a deep, troubled sleep, tossing and turning even just minutes after she at last nodded off.

He held her hand for a moment longer before launching to his feet and tearing silently across the landing, straining his ears as he passed his parents' bedroom, listening for any sound whatsoever. Hearing nothing, he continued, and within seconds found himself stood defiantly and demandingly before the mirror in his bedroom, though he wasn't entirely sure why.

His eyes were adjusted to the dark by now, and he could just about make out the birds on the top corners of the mirror, although it took a few more minutes of focussing in the darkness to make out his own face, and even then it was crooked and distorted in the dim reflection.

Hard as he stared however, fierce as he gazed, furious as he silently stormed, nothing the young boy could do would bring back the figure of the previous night, and he stared helplessly back at his own stubborn face.

For hours Johnathan waited, persistent to the very end.

But, nonetheless, he was not rewarded. The reflection standing before him did not change; it was most definitely just him, through and through.

All that he was left with was the remnants of the terrible anger and longing to seek revenge upon

Richard, though of course at this point he still had no proof other than gut instinct.

And besides all else, it probably wasn't even his own gut instinct insisting that his father was responsible.

Alongside that lust for revenge however, lay also another longing. This one was just as powerful, but instead of filling him with hate, this one filled the young boy with a strange and new love for Emily and Maddie. He had always loved them, of course, they were his family. His mother and his sister meant more to him than anything else. And he would have said the same for his father, but not anymore.

This feeling was something altogether different however, though it was completely beyond him, and hard as he tried, he found it to be quite indescribable.

All in all, it was fairly safe to say that Johnathan was confused beyond belief.

The next morning the confusion was still there, but alongside it Johnathan felt as though his senses were heightened far beyond any point they had ever been before. It was as if he was back in the church, at Father Peter's Service, back where all this madness seemed to have begun. Only now, his senses were even more acute, and he felt as though he could have heard a pin drop.

For all intents and purposes, everything was normal, but through Johnathan's gaze, if it even were his own, things most certainly were not.

His father, Richard, awoke and ate and left for work just as per usual. But all throughout breakfast,

Johnathan felt the tension between his parents, invisible though it was. His mother moved stiffly and grimaced whenever she bent or turned or lifted plates and bowls.

Her pain was well disguised, but from Johnathan's eyes this morning it wasn't even close to hidden.

Maddie too noticed that something was amiss, but not between her mother and father, but with her brother, and her misplaced worry centred on him all morning. Having seen him veiled the day before, she barely took her eyes from him, though she said nothing of it.

When Richard left for work he kissed Emily goodbye and smiled and bade them all farewell, with not another word. On the surface that was fine, but nothing escaped Johnathan's attention that morning, and he saw his mother stiffen horribly when her husband kissed her, and he almost even felt the disgust and the fear pulsating from her as Richard closed the door behind him.

Before long it was time for Maddie and Johnathan to leave also, and the second they stepped beyond the threshold of their home, seemingly indifferent to all other eyes on them now, Maddie's barrage of questions began.

She was unrelenting, finding every chink in Johnathan's armour in every way that only she knew.

"What's going on Johnathan?" She opened. Perhaps not the most tactful approach, but undoubtedly efficient.

"I don't…" He began instinctively, attempting a dumfounded cover.

But this time it wasn't going to work.

"No!" His sister cut him short. "I'm nine! Not stupid!" She promptly informed him, stamping her feet as she walked. "I saw you yesterday! It happened again! You scared me! I want to know what going on!"

Her statements and demands flowed one after another off what seemed to be a single breath.

"Maddie…I really don't…" Johnathan attempted, but again she wouldn't let him finish.

"Tell me!!" She demanded.

Johnathan sighed deeply, finally conceding, though he had little more to tell her that she didn't already know.

"You're right." He admitted. "It happened again yesterday. But I still don't know what it is…"

"Why did it happen again?" Maddie immediately asked, cutting right through to the precise point Johnathan had been attempting to skirt around.

"I don't know, I can't control it…" He half lied. "But you stopped it yesterday. How? What did you do?"

His sister's forehead creased for a moment before she answered.

"I don't know…" She finally replied.

He breathed an inward sigh of relief at having avoided telling her what he'd seen.

"I didn't do anything…" Maddie continued. "I was…I was just there…"

"Well it looks like that's enough." Johnathan replied kindly, smiling a warm smile, comforting his sister.

She hugged him dearly and followed close by him as they approached the school, for they were already nearly there, and all too aware yet again now of the eyes all around upon them.

An hour or so later Maddie caught her brother's eye from across the classroom and stuck her tongue out playfully at him in an attempt to cheer him up. He smiled feebly in response, but quite obviously wasn't as spirited as normal.

He had far too much on his mind.

Johnathan's usual daydreaming was interrupted by a multitude of thoughts.

At that exact moment his wandering mind fell to the conversation he had had with Father Peter, seemingly so long ago now.

'Everybody has demons, Johnathan.'

The old man's words echoed through the young boy's mind.

'That's for you to decide, Johnathan. Our demons are our own.'

And then, for some reason, his thoughts flickered back to the memory of his mother's battered and bruised body, blue and purple and black, and anger and rage boiled up from inside of him once more.

He clenched his fists until they ached and paled white, and sat in a solid, unmoving silence until the end of the day, barely able to contain the rage that felt, as though it wasn't even his.

Johnathan did not speak on the way home, and Maddie walked beside him with concern all too evident in her eyes. His fists remained clenched and did not once relax.

The second they walked in the door Johnathan looked in immediately upon his mother. She sat in the living room, sewing a button back on to one of his father's shirts.

Richard wasn't home yet.

Everything seemed fine.

Relenting his rage slightly, Johnathan tried to breathe deeply. Maddie laid a hand gently on his arm, calming him slightly, and he smiled at her thankfully.

She returned his smile and hugged him tightly before disappearing upstairs to get changed.

Johnathan followed suit, eager to lose the rage he seemed to be holding on to so tightly.

He changed into fresh clothes and washed his face with cold water, attempting to clear his racing thoughts. Then, for some reason, though he didn't imagine it would make his calming any easier, he turned to the mirror and examined his reflection yet again, this time in the still clear light of day.

Breathing heavily, he stared himself dead in the eye, his concentration focused and steady for the first time all day.

For fifteen, if not twenty minutes, he stared at his feeble reflection, frustrated and angry and lost all at the same time.

He heard footsteps shuffle quietly on the landing and glanced away for a second, scanning his gaze towards the door.

Looking back almost immediately, as if he might miss something important, his breath caught in his throat, frozen and terrified.

His reflection was gone, replaced entirely by the figure of another.

A man.

Johnathan simply stared for another minute or two at his changed reflection, entirely dumbfounded.

There was no longer the image of a twelve-year-old boy stood in the mirror, but instead that of a fully grown man.

He was tall, taller than Johnathan, and broad and looked very strong. His eyes were dark, like his hair, and they had a lifetime of experiences behind their gaze, both good and bad.

The man said nor did nothing. He only looked back at Johnathan as he stared, the young boy's mouth agape.

Who was this man?

He looked just like him.

The similarity was uncanny, chilling Johnathan to the bone, and he felt all of a sudden as though he was having a vision into the future.

Was he looking at himself when he was older?

That was impossible, he thought.

Wasn't it…?

The man's frame was broad and powerful, and his wide shoulders and thick arms looked as though they housed the strength of ten men. He wore baggy brown trousers, made from thick, rugged material, and what looked to be sturdy, black boots. His thick, collared shirt was ripped and stained here and there, and the sleeves were rolled up to his elbows, revealing his hands and forearms, strong and battered and bruised and covered in cuts and grazes.

In his one hand he held a weathered, brown leather jacket, faded by time and clearly very well worn.

Johnathan studied the man's face in more detail then, and saw almost immediately that this was indeed the figure he'd seen in the mirror the other night.

Staring into this stranger's eyes, he saw, as he had done before, only now much more clearly, a haunting familiarity, as if he knew this man, or at least should have known him.

But, hard as he tried, as close as his recognition came, Johnathan didn't know him.

"Who are you?" Johnathan eventually mustered up the courage to ask, though the words crept out in only a whisper.

The man only smiled in response at first. He looked as much relieved as he did anything else, and crossed his arms slowly in front of him, folding his faded leather jacket in with them, and his huge shoulders pulled at his loose shirt.

"Johnathan…" Was all the young boy's reflection said to begin with.

It was the first time Johnathan had heard him speak. His voice was deep and rocky and, strangely, thick with love and adoration.

"Who are you?" Johnathan repeated, a little surer of himself this time, though unsure what else to say.

The man smiled again before he replied and tilted his head slightly to one side.

"Arthur." He told Johnathan then, as if assuring the young boy that he meant no harm.

In fact, quite the opposite.

"My name is Arthur."

"Okay…" Johnathan started, his forehead furrowing now with even more questions than before. "But, who are you…?"

The reflection that called itself Arthur laughed softly then, though the sound was deep and coarse, and he looked at Johnathan fondly.

"Don't worry." He reassured the young boy. "I'm here to help you."

But even as Arthur assured him, every time he spoke, Johnathan felt himself speaking the words also, as if they were one and the same person; as if Arthur was a part of him.

Arthur's face turned very serious then and his expression told Johnathan that what he was about to say was very important.

"You must take care of your mother and your sister…"

"What…?" Johnathan started, but even as he began to speak he raised his hand, and in turn his reflection, Arthur, raised his hand also, to quiet him.

The whole experience was bizarre.

"Look after your mother and sister. Look after them…"

Suddenly then, from seemingly nowhere, the mirror began to fog over, and Johnathan's reflection was shrouded beneath it, concealed from view.

"No! Wait!" Johnathan cried in vain, reaching out as if that would stop it from misting over, but there was noting that could be done.

His reflection was gone.

Arthur was gone.

But then, upon the fogged frosted face of the mirror, before Johnathan's very eyes, his outstretched hand reached forward with a mind of its own, and very slowly, very purposefully, letter by letter, traced three words onto the mirror's cloudy face.

It was clear that the words were not his own, and instead belonged to this Arthur, whoever he was.

But still, nonetheless, it was undoubtedly by his own hand that those three words appeared on the face of the mirror, written upon the frosted glass standing before him.

Johnathan took a step back, his knees trembling and his breath caught in his chest, terrified.

With his hand still outstretched he felt his fingers quivering, for though he had traced the words himself, they certainly did not belong to him, and it seemed that Arthur was more a part of him than he could ever have imagined.

look after them

Chapter Seven

A sudden knock at his bedroom door broke Johnathan's transfixed gaze, startling him into movement once again. He glanced over at the wooden door, for barely even a second, struggling to tear his eyes from the words drawn on the misty mirror.

Almost immediately he looked back, and with that his heart sank, for the words were gone, and the face of the mirror was crystal clear. All besides the dim haziness that he was sure was just his own eyes and nothing else, he stared back at his own reflection.

Arthur was gone.

Wallowing in what could only be described as the disappointment of great loss, Johnathan sighed wearily and answered the door.

"Are you okay?" His sister, Maddie, immediately asked, concern clearly painted across her face.

"Yes, I'm fine." He replied automatically, though his expression and his tone spoke volumes that his words did not.

"What's happened?" She persisted, clearly disbelieving. Something had happened, even in the short time since they'd returned home. She could sense it.

"Nothing Maddie." Her brother tried to reassure her, though falsely admittedly. "I'm just tired…"

"No!" She demanded, stamping her foot, refusing his weak explanation. "That's not it! What's happened!?"

Johnathan took a breath at first, wondering what on Earth would convince his sister. But then, after a moment or two, he exhaled with a deep sigh, giving in to her. She always saw right through him, and besides, he didn't really want to keep this from her.

She was the only one he could talk to about it.

"Come on." He said then, beckoning her into his room.

"What...?" Maddie questioned, but he just hurried her inside with a quick motion of his hand.

Confused, she obeyed, closing the door behind her, at her brother's insistence, and allowed him to stand her in front of his mirror. She knew it had once belonged to her grandfather, but other than that, and the fact that it was pretty, there wasn't really anything special about it.

Maddie stood there for a minute or two, feeling inwardly rather foolish, as her brother looked on expectantly, and she hadn't a clue what he was waiting for.

Eventually she grew impatient.

"What are we looking at?" She finally asked, frowning at her own reflection and glancing up at her brother, standing almost a full foot taller than her.

Her brother frowned then too, disappointment flashing in his eyes, momentarily overtaking all the expectant hope that had filled them just seconds ago.

"I saw a man..." He attempted, examining the mirror ever more closely, running his fingers over it, checking for something, anything, Maddie had no idea what.

But then again, neither did he.

"A man…?" She queried.

"Yes." He confirmed. "It was my reflection. But it wasn't me. He was there instead of my reflection. He looked like me. But I'm sure it wasn't me. I felt like I knew him."

Maddie looked at her brother, admittedly very worried now. He wasn't making any sense.

"Are you okay?" She asked seriously, reaching out for his arm.

"Yes!" He exclaimed. "Maddie I'm fine. I promise you, there was a man…"

"There's no man Johnathan…" His sister said gently, pursing her lips worriedly.

"I'm not crazy Maddie!" He almost begged then, turning to her, admittedly a little crazily. His eyes were slightly wild and confused, as if trying to decide indeed whether or not he was going insane.

Maddie looked at her brother then, pulling him away from the mirror and holding him firmly by the arms.

"Johnathan! What's happened!?" She urged, frightened by her brother's insistence. "Tell me!"

Suddenly then, for some reason, Johnathan's trail of thought flickered to something seemingly entirely unrelated, and words began to tumble from his mouth that he had no control over.

"I'm sorry that I did those things to Brock. I never meant to hurt anybody. I was only trying to protect you. I never meant to scare you. I would never want to scare you…"

Maddie opened her mouth to reply, admittedly a little taken aback. Then she closed and opened it again, not knowing quite what to say.

Eventually, deciding it would make no difference what she said, one way or another, she sighed and hugged her big brother tightly, wrapping her arms around him and squeezing with all her nine-year-old might.

"Don't be silly…" She finally whispered, smiling gently with her head rested on her brother's shoulder. "You didn't scare me. I was worried about you, but I know you were only protecting me."

Johnathan said nothing in reply, and only hugged his sister even more tightly. She was truly the only person he had ever always been able to count on, even in their lives so short.

But the falseness in her words, even just the slightest trace of it, he detected, sensing with some morsel of his subconscious the fear that she was hiding. It was nothing malicious, but it was fear nonetheless.

Fear of uncertainty.

Fear of the unknown.

Fear of what was yet to come.

That night the sky purpled and blackened menacingly overhead as the winds whipped themselves into an invisible, blurred frenzy. Its ravenous teeth bit at the exposed leaves on the trees and snapped at the icy surface of the river that struck so piercingly through the innocent little village of Riverbrook.

All around, besides the shrill feet of the wind pattering through the shrub life, not a cry nor a squawk nor a peep could be heard.

So, when the scream rang out through the shrill darkness of the night, single and piercing and desperate, it was heard in eagerness and earnest all around.

Maddie shot bolt upright in her bed, her heart racing and her breaths shallow and frantic.

She was sure she had heard a scream.

She had been dreaming, though for some reason she couldn't recall what about, when the sound had awoken her so abruptly.

Besides the sound of her own breathing however, no matter how hard she strained to listen, she could hear not a sound. All was quiet in the Davies household, and all were sound asleep it seemed.

But something felt not quite right to the young girl. In fact, the sweat on her palms and the shiver that was racing up and down her spine told her that something was terribly wrong.

She crept silently from her bed, rubbing her bare arms from the tingling cold, and tiptoed across her small room, dim and black, to the door allowing in a single beam of light through the slightest of cracks.

Peering carefully with one eye pressed to the gap between the door and its frame, Maddie peeked out onto the landing.

All was still.

She could see perhaps a few feet in each direction, and just to the top of the wooden staircase that led downstairs.

There she stayed for a few minutes, not really knowing quite what she was looking for, but looking all the same.

Perhaps it had been nothing after all.

Maybe the sound that had woken her had actually been part of her dreams?

Suddenly a figure loomed in front of her, blocking her view and startling the wits from her tiny frame. She reeled back and clasped her hands over her mouth. It was all she could do to keep from screaming in fright.

Whatever it was blocked most of the light that crept in through the crack, and cast her into almost total darkness.

For a moment terror consumed the young girl, and all manner of horrible thoughts fleeted through her mind.

But then, just as suddenly as the figure had appeared, it vanished, and her racing heart quietened ever so slightly.

From somewhere deep within her then, Maddie plucked up the courage to creep back over to the door again, and once again peeked out onto the landing, holding her breath tightly. She looked left first and saw nothing, but then glanced right and immediately laid eyes upon the figure that had sprung up so terrifyingly before her.

It was Johnathan!

She exhaled with heavy relief and pulled the door slowly open. It moved with an almost inaudible creak, but of course her brother heard it, and he whipped round in barely a moment to face her, his eyes fierce in the dim light.

Maddie froze and her breath caught in her chest yet again, for some reason fearful even still.

When he saw that it was his sister who had startled him, Johnathan's eyes softened slightly, but even in the darkness of the landing, Maddie, scared by what she saw, could see that the expression her brother held wasn't his own.

Johnathan slowly raised a hand and lifted one finger to his lips, motioning for her to stay silent.

She inherently obeyed.

Terrified.

Her brother slowly turned back away from her, standing perfectly still and staring across the landing at their parents' bedroom door.

Still there was only silence, and after a moment Maddie realised she'd been holding her breath and exhaled slowly. Grateful for the release, the stabbing pain in her lungs subsided and her eyes continued to adjust to the sight before her, though yet she didn't understand it any further.

Suddenly another scream pierced the darkness, though this one was more of a stifled cry, and Maddie's heart almost leapt from her chest. Her stomach knotted horribly in both shock and fright, and it took her a few seconds to recover before she managed to stir her young body into action.

"Mother!" She cried, rushing forwards, careering around her brother, still stood motionless and unmoving on the landing, and she almost threw herself against her parents' bedroom door.

Immediately she tried the handle, but the door was locked, and almost in the same moment as she tried it, she heard her mother's heavy wooden dresser being pushed in front of the door, blocking any chance she might have had of opening it.

"No! Mother! NO!!" Maddie screamed then, banging her fists against the door in a sudden frenzy, petrified, not knowing what was happening.

All of a sudden another shriek rang out from beyond the locked, barricaded door, shrill and afraid and desperate.

"No! Please!" Emily's despairing voice begged from beyond the blockade.

Her words were fraught with danger and all the strength and fight seemed drained from them, as if years of abuse had worn them down; as if there was simply not enough will left in her to fight any longer.

Silence pierced the night again then. Maddie strained her ears against the deafening quiet, and strained her body against the immovable door, pushing with all her might, but not able to budge it even an inch.

A creaking floorboard shattered the soundless darkness then, and Maddie whipped her head around, only to almost leap from her skin yet again. She yelped and choked as she turned to face her brother, his face barely inches from her own.

"J...Jo...Johnathan!!" She cried and spluttered, trying desperately to find her petrified words. "Do something!"

But Johnathan didn't reply.

He stared at her almost blankly for a moment, before slowly raising his gaze above his sister's head and staring coldly at the door to their parents' bedroom.

"Johnathan…?" Maddie started, fear overwhelming her now.

His eyes were level and serious.

Whoever he was, whatever he was thinking, he wasn't her brother.

Maddie backed away slowly, moving to one side and out of his line of sight, terrified beyond belief.

But her movement drew his attention yet again, and the figure that looked like Maddie's brother, but wasn't, turned back to her. The veil had well and truly descended over him, and as he advanced upon her, looming above her, Maddie once again held her breath tight and squeezed her eyes closed, horrified of what was to come.

However, regardless of what she'd expected, she hadn't a clue, what happened next astonished her.

She felt her brother, or his body at least, wrap its kind arms around her, and in that moment, it was as if Maddie regained something that she had lost so long ago, and in some strange way, she felt almost a step closer to being whole again.

The young girl hugged the figure tightly back, for a second feeling somehow entirely safe and secure and content.

The way a girl so young should feel.

And then it passed, and the fear returned. The figure gently released her and eased her back slightly, away from the barricaded door, looked at her for a second with its level and steady and terrifying gaze, a gaze that saw right through her, and then turned away.

As it took a step closer to the door, Maddie was convinced for a second that the figure before her was no longer a boy, but instead a full grown man, for it loomed tall and powerful, though of course that was impossible.

Her brother's body placed its outstretched hand on the door to their parents' bedroom, resting its fingertips gently upon the wooden face. Nothing else happened for a moment, and the silence cut through the air like a blade with murderous intent.

Maddie's thoughts raced, yet said nothing, all at once. All she could comprehend was the dark silhouette of her brother in the dim light.

Then the muffled sound of a cry escaped the quiet all around, creeping meekly through the barricade before them, followed by the sickening sounds of a heavy smack and a dull thud.

A sharp gasp completed the deathly sequence.

It was undoubtedly their mother, of that Maddie was certain, and tears coursed down her cheeks involuntarily.

And then she saw Johnathan change, unmistakeably. Even in the dark of the night, it was all too obvious. If he hadn't been her brother before, he most definitely wasn't now.

She saw it descend upon him as if another person took over his body completely, and in that moment her dear brother became something that the young girl did not know, but somehow also, strangely, at the same time, something that she recognised.

But there was no time for her to decipher what she saw, for Johnathan's veiling was complete within seconds, though it felt like long, torturous decades, and his fingertips resting upon the door slowly clenched into a fist, resting its knuckles against the hard, offensive, abusive wood.

Then the onslaught began.

With the strength of a man, though it seemed that in his terrible rage Johnathan had even the strength of a great bear.

He smashed his fists into the wooden door before him, catching the doorframe too with his mighty blows, shattering and splintering wood in all directions, splitting the door almost directly in two as it buckled and divided and screamed beneath his mighty rain of blows.

Maddie sheltered her eyes from the shards spraying all over the place, raising her arms to protect herself.

As the door turned to splinters, the heavy dresser beyond it was revealed, but that too was no match for the man stood before Maddie now. The figure that once was her brother didn't even bother to pummel the massive dresser to pieces. He simply placed his hands at the base of it, catching the bottom lip with his fingertips, and with inhuman strength and simply impossible ease, lifted the massive oaken cupboard and launched it across the bedroom, smashing it into the wall at the opposite end of the room.

It exploded into a million shattered pieces that careered off in every direction, spraying them all with its fallout.

"WHAT THE…!?" Richard started, yelling with both anger and shock.

But before he could finish, the man that stood in the place of Johnathan stormed through the shattered doorway to face him.

The tension that radiated all around then was something to be rivalled, and the sight that beheld Maddie when she followed her protector through and into her parents' bedroom sent her knees weak and cast great sobs from her chest.

Their mother lay upon the now splinter covered floor, shaking and writhing weakly, bleeding, her nightclothes ripped and torn and tattered and stained red.

Johnathan too beheld the sight, no longer entirely as a man that Maddie didn't know, but at least partly as himself, and disgust rippled through his body like a great wave.

Emily glanced up in horror to see her children, or at the very least one of them, revealing her face freshly bruised and tarnished. Tears streaked openly down her cheeks as she opened her mouth, straining desperately to speak, but no sound came out, and her chest and ribs heaved and strained in agony.

Emily Davies looked entirely broken and defeated; as if there was no physical pain that she could possibly suffer worse than the emotional torment she was already living.

She was a broken woman.

Maddie's so-called father however, Richard Davies, stood by the side of the bed, fists clenched also. He was topless, and his scrawny, exposed chest was cut and grazed and bleeding by scratches staining his skin here and there across his torso.

His eyes were not wild, as one might have expected, but instead focused and concise and purposeful.

There was no love here.

There was only cruelty and hatred.

There was only evil.

Chapter Eight

"WHAT THE HELL DO YOU THINK YOU'RE DOING!!??" Richard Davies bellowed with all his might, almost shaking the walls with his voice alone, reigning with terror alone it seemed.

It was perhaps the most fearsome his pathetic frame had ever been.

Without waiting for a reply, the evil man reached out for Johnathan's throat, imagining the life draining from him even before he had reached his target.

"RICHARD NO!!!" Emily screamed up from the floor, still unable to move, but dredging every last morsel of strength she had left to try to protect her children from this monster.

It didn't help though, and still Richard advanced, barely moments away, and still the figure that had once been Johnathan had not moved.

Finding desperate strength from somewhere, God only knows where, Emily exploded up from the floor. It was desperation found only in natural parental instinct.

She launched herself into her husband's side and knocked him away with all her remaining strength, throwing him off balance for a few precious seconds, sending him reeling over the already bloodstained bed.

"Go Johnathan!!" His mother hissed to him, dropping to her knees in exhaustion, but reaching out for him in desperation, wild, crazed fear and despair in her eyes. "Take Maddie!!" She urged. "Go!! Find Father Peter!!"

But that was all there was time for her to say before her husband was once again upon her, this time most definitely filled with rage.

He grabbed her from behind by her hair and she screamed wildly and involuntarily, clutching at his wrist too powerful to fight, her hands too weak to resist.

Richard raised his free hand and paused for a moment, holding his wife off the ground still by her hair. He looked across to their children, Johnathan and Maddie.

The girl was trembling and terrified, as he expected, but the boy was unmoving and unemotional.

The look in his eyes was almost unnatural, and it scared Richard, for it was a look he had only ever seen once before.

"What the hell is wrong with you, boy!?" He demanded of Johnathan, covering his fear with as strong a façade as he could manage. "Get out of my sight!!" He ordered.

And with that he brought his heavy hand down with a sharp crack and struck his wife square across the face. He released his firm grip on her hair as he did so and she crumpled heavily to the floor.

Maddie let out an involuntary sob, and it was suddenly all too much for Johnathan.

His sister saw his body shudder and felt something change in the air all around him once again.

She had thought for a moment she had him back, after he had broken through the door, but soon enough she knew he would be gone again.

The change lasted but a mere second or two, but she felt it nonetheless. The space that Johnathan had occupied in the room, his frame tiny in comparison to their father's, suddenly was not filled with the body nor aura of a terrified twelve-year-old.

Instead, his aura spread and morphed and evolved, and before long all three of them could feel it. Stood in Johnathan's place, though physically he had not changed, was certainly not a young boy, or even the remnants of one, but a different person altogether.

The change was even more drastic than before, and Maddie's heart felt as though it would explode from her chest.

"Johnathan…?" His little sister whispered, clinging to the hope that he might still be there somewhere. Or, at least, that was what she'd clung to before.

But this time she knew her words were futile, for it was most certainly no longer even partly her brother that stood before them now.

Who was it?

Whomever the aura belonged to, however, it felt familiar to Maddie, yet she could not for the life of her place it.

Maddie's mother, Emily, looked up from the floor then, seemingly with new hope pooling in her eyes, shrouded by thick, pain stricken tears. Though now, undoubtedly, her gaze was dashed with newfound courage, stirred up by something, rather than simply desperation and defeat.

"It can't be…" She whispered, just loud enough for Maddie to hear. "How…"

"What the…!?" Richard started again, but he was not given the opportunity to finish that sentence.

The man who stood in Johnathan's place exploded forward in a sudden flurry of movement and crashed into Richard's chest. The impact sent him reeling backward as if a bull had struck him.

Recovering slowly, clutching his battered ribs, Richard clambered sluggishly to his feet. He finally found his footing and charged forwards, swinging a heavy fist toward the man's unprotected face, but again, with seemingly unparalleled experience, the unknown figure ducked and blocked and weaved as a flurry of blows were thrown at him.

Eventually, after not all that long, in his fatigue, Richard exposed a weakness, and his opponent immediately exploited the opening.

A sharp kick to the side of Richard's leg dropped him to one knee, and from there he was surely finished.

Driving his knee heavily into the side of Richard's ribs, forcing the air from his lungs, Johnathan, or whoever he was, was in complete control. A quick strike to the side of Richard's neck sent his eyes rolling in their sockets, and the victor raised his hand high above his head to deliver what even Maddie knew would be the final blow.

The young girl held her breath until her lungs burned and felt as though they would burst, but still she was too petrified to move.

"Arthur…?" Maddie's mother whispered then, trembling from where she lay on the floor.

The sound of her voice broke the heavy tension in the room, and the walls all around seemed to heave a huge sigh of relief.

Suddenly the man who stood in Johnathan's place relaxed his grip on Richard, and his furious, clenched fist loosed and opened. He allowed Emily's supposed husband to slide limply to the floor, unconscious, but alive.

The figure stood where her son should have been turned then to Emily with love in his eyes, and Maddie could see even from where she stood, shaking, frozen and terrified, that the look in his eyes and the expression on his face were not her brother's.

Nonetheless though, whomever they belonged to, it was clear that they loved and cherished and cared for her mother with all their heart.

The man who stood in Johnathan's place, although fully grown, yet somehow at the same time still merged with the meagre body of a twelve-year-old, knelt beside Emily and scooped her gently into his arms.

He lifted her effortlessly from the ground and held her close, shaking slightly, though Maddie somehow sensed that it was not out of fear, but instead great relief.

Emily buried her head immediately into his shoulder and fresh tears streamed down her cheeks.

He turned and placed her tenderly down on the bed.

Cupping her cheek in his hand for a moment, he looked deeply into her eyes and tears coursed down both of their cheeks openly.

Emily smiled then: a genuine smile of happiness long lost that brought a twinge of pain to even Maddie's heart, for she had never seen such a look in her mother's eyes.

Then, as if knowing he had very little time left, the man kissed Emily lovingly on her forehead and turned away, walking immediately over towards Maddie.

The young's girl's mother said nothing, but the look on her face as he turned to their daughter was one of both total adoration, and at the same time terrible loss.

Her hand reached out involuntarily after him, longing for him to return.

The man that was Johnathan, and then also at the same time most certainly not her brother, placed his hands softly on Maddie shoulders then, kneeling down to looked her adoringly in the eye.

Seeing him up so close now, Maddie racked her brain to think who this man was. Though it might have been her brother's face and body, still clearly it wasn't. Yet still, as she had realised earlier, she still felt as though she already knew this man.

He smiled then and kissed her lightly on her forehead, just as he had done to her mother. Pulling her gently into an embrace, Maddie accepted it, for some reason willingly, and held him tightly, feeling warm and safe and complete once more.

They pulled each other close and Emily smiled and even let out a joyful sob.

Then all of a sudden he shuddered, as if he feared that his time was up.

Fresh tears streaked down his face again as he released Maddie, holding on to her for as long as he possibly could.

He cast one quick fleeting, and admittedly longing glance back at Emily, before immediately tearing his streaming eyes from her and departing.

Vanishing from the bedroom and away into the darkness, the man that was Johnathan disappeared, merging amongst the shadows of the night, leaving his Emily and Maddie alone.

They looked at each other for a moment, both in shock and amazement, but it was only for a second or two before Maddie tore across the ruined bedroom and leapt into her mother's arms, and the both of them sobbed and heaved with terror and fright and relief.

Chapter Nine

Raindrops heavy with sin and regret fell thunderously down from the pitch black skies, smeared grey and blurred by clouds filled to the brim. It was as if the night had been hanging precariously upon a single thread, and even the slightest movement either way would tip the balance.

Johnathan's head spun as the cold night's air whipped about his face and body. He blinked awake, his eyes weighty and painful, almost as if he had been concentrating too hard. Feeling groggy, as though he had just awoken from a deep sleep, the young boy brought his hands up to his face and rubbed his eyes.

His hands were cold and his fingertips were chapped.

As his senses began to return to him, Johnathan realised exactly how cold he was, and as he glanced around and shivered violently, he saw exactly why.

He found that he was stood alone outside, in the middle of the night, and though the ground beneath his feet was still relatively dry, the heavens above had not long opened, in more ways than one, and the new, fresh rainfall was stealing the warmth from his skin.

The bewildered young boy saw also then that, not only was he outside, surrounded by strange darkness, but that he was stood directly before Father Peter's church, staring up at its great, looming silhouette in the dim of the night.

Of course, it was not, strictly speaking, Father Peter's church, Johnathan thought to himself then. It belonged to the people, both to those who still lived, and to those who didn't. Or, at least, that was how the young boy envisioned it to be, in his mind, in this bizarre situation he found himself in.

The vibrant stained glass windows stretched high above him. Their usual warm glow was absent, leaving the images they cast dark and cold and empty. The morning had barely begun after all, and Johnathan imagined that Father Peter would be sleeping soundly at this hour.

But oh how wrong he was.

Within what seemed like only seconds, the heavy doors that marked the main entrance to the church, groaned and creaked slowly open. A nervous, flickering candle came into view, carried upon a silver bowl.

The dancing light illuminated Father Peter's outline and face, decorated as per usual by his long, thick robes. His tired eyes were weary with deep concern and responsibility. Although, in seeing Johnathan, his worry seemed to dissipate slightly, and a brief expression housing relief flitted across his aged face.

He seemed to have been expected Johnathan.

Without even the need for beckoning, Johnathan's body seemed to respond automatically, and his legs carried him forwards. Father Peter stepped aside without as much as a word, allowing the boy to enter, and closed the door behind him with a loud bang, only amplified by the night engulfing them.

Still carried by his legs, seemingly without a thought, Johnathan heeded Father Peter's silent wishes and walked around to the pew closest to the lectern at the front of the nave, as the Vicar set about lighting the candles nearest to where Johnathan had taken his seat.

Finally, after what felt like decades, the old man finished lighting all the candles it seemed that he deemed necessary for whatever was about to come, and sidled along to take a seat in the pew next to the young boy.

There was an eerie déjà vu to the scene, and Johnathan couldn't help but shudder.

"Johnathan…" Father Peter began almost immediately, his voice soft and careful and admittedly even cautious.

This was the first time there hadn't been an abrupt silence to begin their conversation.

"Father Peter…" He replied, not knowing what else to say, staring numbly at the Vicar, overwhelmed.

Father Peter sighed deeply then and rubbed his ancient face wearily.

"I have been praying for you of late, my boy…" He offered then, revealing the fact that he perhaps knew more about everything that had happened recently than Johnathan did, but nothing else. "I know you have been struggling lately…"

His guise had the desired effect however, and Johnathan seemed to focus more keenly for a moment, as if a spark had just suddenly ignited.

"Do you know what's happening to me?" Johnathan asked then. "What's going on?"

"I know it's been difficult, Johnathan…" The Vicar started, buffering the truth. But Johnathan didn't want to hear it.

"No!" He the young boy suddenly demanded, most uncharacteristically. "What's happening to me!?"

"I don't know John…"

"NO!" Johnathan cut him off again with a shrill cry, rising suddenly to his feet as his voice boomed and echoed around the great, stone hall. "TELL ME!!"

"Johnath…" The Vicar attempted again, but again unsuccessfully.

"NO!!!" The young boy yelled, stepping menacingly closer to the old man, fear and anger in his eyes.

"JOHNATHAN!!" Father Peter suddenly bellowed, exploding to his feet, his great voice not so much reverberating around the massive chamber as much as completely filling it. There was fear in his eyes also, but it was driven by uncertainty more so than anger.

They stared at each other in the dim, flickering light for a moment, both unsure of what the other was going to do, until, after a few more moments, Johnathan finally cracked.

The young boy's shoulders and chest heaved slightly, almost unnoticeably at first, though it was enough for the old man to know what was coming next.

Within seconds, Johnathan's barriers crumbled and he collapsed in tears into Father Peter's awaiting arms, protective and secure in these times of terror and uncertainty.

Between mumbled sobs Johnathan tried to speak, even to apologise, but it took several attempts for him to finally string together anything remotely coherent.

"He…He was…He was beating her…" He eventually managed. "He…I…I had to…I'm sorry…He was…What do I…" His words descended as another wave of guilt ridden panic swept over him, and he shook evermore violently with every sob.

Father Peter did not reply at first, and simply held the young boy, understanding his pain, having felt similar such a wrench many times himself in his time, and waited patiently for it to pass. At least now he hoped the danger of an immediate recurrence was passed also.

After quite some time, the worst of Johnathan's grief faded, and Father Peter sat him down again in the pews.

"Do you remember the story I told once Johnathan…" Father Peter began then, seeming to change tact completely. His voice carried a tone of bemusement, worry and contemplation, somehow all in one, and Johnathan's curiosity, admittedly amidst his sorrow, peaked slightly.

"Story?" The young boy questioned before the old man could finish, having found his voice again by now.

"About how Riverbrook was founded?" He finished simply, raising a curved, grey eyebrow slightly at his young audience.

"You said a traveller was lost." Johnathan started, closing his eyes as if to visualise the tale he had been told and remember it. "He found a river, followed it, stopped here, and built the village." He summed his recollection up then. "Other people came too…" He added then. "And he got married and they had children."

"Very concise." Father Peter kindly commended him. "But he had never been lost."

"Sorry?" Johnathan questioned, confused.

"He had never been lost." The old man repeated.

"But you said…?"

"No…" The old man corrected him gently then. "I said he didn't know where he was. I knew him, Johnathan, and he was a great man. He always knew exactly where he was going, even if he didn't know where he was."

That didn't really make much sense to Johnathan, and his forehead creased in thought.

"But they're the same thing, aren't they?" He eventually asked, but the old Vicar shook his head with a warm, kindly smile.

"No, my boy. They most certainly are not."

Johnathan did not ask another question straight away then, for he was perplexed by the old man's words.

They did not make sense to him in the slightest.

It's impossible to know where you're going, if you don't know where you are, he thought.

Surely?

Finally, after much silent deliberation, he finally piped up another question: the only one that really seemed relevant.

"Why?" He asked.

"Why what?" The Vicar replied, as if playing some sort of game.

Johnathan knew he knew what he meant, but he answered him anyway.

"Why did you ask me if I remembered the story?"

"Because…" The old man started, though clearly he was deep in thought, as if carefully considering his answer. He finally continued. "If you didn't, I wouldn't be able to tell you what I'm about to tell you."

"Why not?" Johnathan immediately asked, and almost just as immediately, the old man broke into laughter.

Johnathan was very confused by this point.

"What's funny?" He questioned, admittedly a little hurt, feeling as though the old man was poking fun at him.

"Nothing, my boy, nothing." The old man assured him, coughing to clear his throat and sighing, though quite joyfully. "I'm not laughing at you. It's just, anybody else would have asked what I was going to tell them, not why I couldn't."

"Isn't why you do, or don't do something, just as important as what you do?" The young boy immediately replied, and Father Peter practically beamed back at him, almost as if that question was momentous beyond belief.

"You would make your father very proud." The old man said suddenly then, and a thick lump caught in Johnathan's throat, taken aback by the comment, and he felt physically sick to the stomach.

Shock held him for a moment, but then that shock dissipated entirely, and his expression turned into a fierce and vicious scowl.

"I am nothing like him." The boy replied, his voice heavy and low like thunder.

"And that's exactly why I wouldn't have been able to tell you…" The old Vicar replied.

Johnathan's glare remained, but he said nothing, allowing the old man to continue.

"Richard is not your father, Johnathan."

The shock returned then, tenfold, and this time its grasp was unshakeable.

Johnathan blinked and his mouth hung slightly agape, but not words, nor or even thoughts, would come to him.

"My boy, your father, your real father, was named Arthur Knight, and he founded Riverbrook."

Now there was most certainly no chance of words finding their way from Johnathan's tongue, even though countless questions raced through his mind. But Father Peter seemed to sense this, and simply gave the boy the answer he knew he needed.

"Your father founded the village, in exactly the way I told everyone in my Service. And, also, just as I said, after some time, your mother was drawn here too."

Johnathan's eyes were focused so intently on the Vicar by this point that he barely even blinked.

"Arthur was a good man, a great man in fact. And he was very wealthy, but your mother didn't marry him for his money. She married him because she loved him; she loved him dearly, and he loved her so too."

Father Peter paused then, though his breath was drawn, and it was as if his next words would deliver such a terrible blow that he almost dared not say them. But regardless, he was committed now, and the answer next to leave his lips was the one Johnathan so desperately sought above all others.

"Your father was killed, Johnathan." The old Vicar said then, exhaling deeply and with fretful eyes.

Johnathan's fists clenched. The hairs on his arms and the back of his neck stood perfectly straight, and his whole body pimpled with goose bumps, but still he neither moved nor spoke. His eyes continued to bore into the old man, their dark gaze hard and cold as stone.

"Your mother was devastated." The old Vicar continued cautiously, though that much at least was obvious. "But I cared for her as much as I could. She came here often: every day to begin with, for her grief was awful. I honestly at one point even thought it might be endless. I had never seen such a thing."

Still Johnathan's gaze remained unchanged and Father Peter swallowed nervously, but he continued.

"Of course then all of your father's wealth became hers, but she didn't care about that. She had you and your sister. You were both too young to remember I imagine. And all the money in the world wouldn't replace your father."

He smiled then, as if remembering all the good things about this man whom Johnathan had never known.

The thought of it hurt the young boy deeply, but he knew it wasn't the old man's fault. He had done everything he possibly could.

"He was a brave man, Johnathan." Father Peter continued. "A great man. A kind man. A Knight in fact, just as you are. A Knight, both in the way you protect your family, and in the goodness of your heart."

"Who killed him?" The young boy suddenly asked, finding enough voice from deep inside of him to ask that single burning question.

But Father Peter's lips tightened and his eyes dropped. Johnathan sighed and simply accepted what he had expected.

"We never found out..." The old man finally admitted, though his words came in barely even a whisper. "His body was found dumped by the river. I tried to be there for your mother, like I said. But it wasn't enough. She became very ill."

"Ill?" Johnathan questioned, concern in his voice.

"It wasn't her body that was sick." The Vicar tried to explain. "It was her mind."

"How can that be?" The young boy asked, worried for his mother.

"Her sadness became too much. It overwhelmed her. I tried desperately to help her. But it seemed that it didn't matter what I did, she just kept getting worse."

"How did you make her better?"

"I didn't." Father Peter admitted again then.

"What do you mean you didn't? She got better, didn't she?" Johnathan's concern was building more quickly than he could control it, but Father's Peter next words knocked him yet again.

"I didn't make her better. Richard did…"

"What…?" Johnathan breathed, his voice dripping with undisguised venom.

"He appeared one day, from the far south, drawn to Riverbrook I imagine like most people here have been. I wasn't entirely happy; he was a stranger after all. But he cared for your mother, and seemed to heal her, even if only slightly. So I didn't intervene. It wasn't my place to."

The Vicar's voice dropped as he explained what had happened, as if somehow he was ashamed of his actions.

"Soon enough your mother stopped coming to see me so regularly, and not long after they approached me and asked me to wed them. I still wasn't sure, and such a thing is almost unheard of, but they both seemed to be happy, so of course I did."

"That was it?" Johnathan blurted out then, stubbornness and resentment in his tone. "They just got married and forgot about my father!?" But Father Peter cut him short very quickly.

"No, Johnathan." His voice was firm and steadfast, reproachful even. "Richard did not replace your father. Your mother has never been the same again. He was just there when she needed someone."

"And what about now!?" Johnathan demanded, and of course they both knew to what he was referring.

The old man sighed deeply and his shoulders seemed to weigh down with a burden that had lasted for many long, hard years.

"No one knows who killed your real father." He said then, sorrowfully. "Many believed that he was simply mugged…"

"But you don't…" Johnathan perceived.

"No." The Vicar agreed. "You're right. I don't. Arthur was a strong man. And he was well versed in, well, pretty much everything. He built Riverbrook from the ground up, not alone, admittedly, but he had a hand in it all. There wasn't anything he couldn't do, and that included being able to fight…"

"So what do you believe?" The young boy asked, almost pleading, leaning closer, gripping the edge of the wooden pew upon which he sat so hard that his knuckles faded white.

"As time has gone on, and especially now more recently, I fear perhaps that the mugging myth may not be true."

"Why?" Johnathan urged him to continue, and the old man looked deep in thought. His eyes narrowed as if even what he was thinking was absurd, even though he knew it was the truth.

"I have felt the presence of your father for some time now, more strongly than I ever have done since he was killed. But I didn't know what it meant…"

Johnathan said nothing, but the look in his eyes and the cold expression on his face begged the Vicar for more information.

"Arthur's presence worries me. If there was ever trouble, or danger, or worry, he was never far away. He always seemed to know, somehow, regardless of who it was affecting. He was just that kind of person. He was a protector. And I see no reason why his death would have changed that fact."

"But he's dead." Johnathan declared. "How could he possibly know?"

"He's dead Johnathan, not gone." The old Vicar corrected him.

"They're the same thing." Johnathan disagreed, and for not the first time in that conversation.

But Father Peter shook his head and smiled ruefully.

"They're not." He said gently. "And that's the problem…"

"What do you mean?" Johnathan asked, confused again.

This was all getting too much for him now.

"After what's happened to your mother…The things Richard has done…I fear he may never have loved her…" The old man sighed and rubbed his weary eyes, for they were heavy from burden and from lack of sleep.

The very early light of morning was slowly creeping its way over the horizon, for they had been there for hours by now, and it was slowly beginning to flood the vast hall with streams of light coloured by the tall windows.

"I fear he may only have married her for your father's money…" He continued. "He took advantage of her when she was most vulnerable…"

Johnathan did not reply.

"No one in the village knew of your family's wealth. Arthur never flaunted it, and I know he would have gladly given much of it away over seeing others suffer or struggle. But then, unfortunately, such acts of generosity rarely go unnoticed, for they are in themselves a rarity..."

"But if no one in the village knew about my father's money, and if Richard didn't even live in the village, how on Earth did he know? He wouldn't even have known my mother had been married." Johnathan reasoned, and indeed his logic was sound.

"Hmm..." Came Father Peter's only reply, contemplating, considering the boy's words, though there was obvious distraught in his eyes, as if he had asked himself the same questions a thousand times.

And then the terrible truth struck Johnathan full force, for he was not stupid, and the great blow knocked the wind from his lungs and his stomach felt as though it had turned inside out.

"He didn't...He can't have...He...No..." The young boy gasped, clutching at the pew, at his stomach, at his chest, anything to make the pain stop.

But there was nothing.

He reeled over, collapsing to his hands and knees upon the floor, and simply screamed and roared until his throat was raw and his voice croaked, unable to scream any longer.

And then, finally, when there was no more sound to be had, and the blind, furious anger seemed to have passed, he simply sat and shook and sobbed upon the cold, harsh floor.

Long through the early hours of the morning until well past the sunrise that had already begun, Johnathan grieved, and there was absolutely nothing Father Peter could do to comfort him, besides let the young boy's anguish run its course.

But then, as the old man sadly knew, all too well, the grief would slowly fade, and the anger would return, fouled evermore so by bitterness and hatred.

Just as Arthur had once been, Father Peter could see in Johnathan his father's desperate desire to protect his family: to keep them from harm.

Johnathan left the church that new morning much less of a boy, and much more of a man.

And not just any man at that, but indeed truly a Knight, brave and strong and determined.

Chapter Ten

Everything seemed normal. Or, at least, anyone on the outside looking in may have at first mistaken that morning for an ordinary one.

On second glance however, it was painfully obvious that that was most certainly not the case.

Johnathan had not slept, for he had not long arrived back, and he had told no one about his visit with Father Peter. In fact, no one had spoken at all. The house was filled with an eerie silence as the four of them shuffled about in a manner most unnatural.

The young boy's tired eyes were everywhere as he sat at the table in the kitchen, but most of all they bore fiercely into the man he had for almost his entire life known as his father.

But Richard Davies was a father to him no more.

Glancing across for a brief second at his mother and sister, Johnathan's heart skipped a beat, as it did every time, as his gaze came to rest ever so briefly on their faces.

His sister looked terrified, almost completely beyond belief, and his mother's face was bruised and purpled from the night previous. Though, hidden amidst that bruising, as she looked up briefly and caught her son's gaze, her eyes were not entirely lost, and they seemed to be searching for something in Johnathan's expression that he didn't quite understand.

He snapped his eyes back to Richard as the dreadful man rose from the table, having finished his breakfast, going about his morning as per usual, totally ignoring the three of them.

It did bring a slight, sly smile to Johnathan lips however as he noted that the terrible man moved stiffly, grunting as he bent and twisted even slightly, his hands reaching involuntarily to clutch here and there at his leg, his ribs, his neck. Clearly he was suffering, and that satisfied Johnathan somewhat, but it was nowhere near enough.

What his so-called father had done was unforgivable.

Nonetheless, the frightful man gathered his things and prepared to leave for work, not once looking at any of them.

Johnathan felt sick to the stomach as he watched him go, realising all of a sudden that he had believed, for all these years, with such naïve trust, that the man he had called father, Richard Davies, had been working so as to provide for his family.

Their lives: their safety and their happiness and their security, had all been so because of him, because he loved them.

But no.

All this time he had been stealing from Johnathan's mother. And he had killed his father to do it.

Johnathan seethed silently.

Of course the young boy, so full of rage, had no evidence to prove this either way, but the dreadful feeling in his gut, in his very core, was all the evidence he needed.

It was not the first time he had gone on gut instinct alone, and he had yet to be proven wrong.

Sometimes that deep, gut feeling can be a mixed blessing or a disguised sin however, and unfortunately the young boy Johnathan Knight was, at that moment in time, far too young to even begin to know the difference.

Maddie walked closer by Johnathan's side than ever that morning it seemed, and her eyes were cast down to the ground and almost perpetually brimmed with tears. Occasionally Johnathan put his arm gently around his little sister's shoulder, as if to reassure her that everything would be alright, but they did not speak.

There was nothing to say.

Johnathan's eyes were still everywhere at once, and he felt strangely alert, as if he knew he was watching for something, anything. He was silent and focused, thinking only of Richard and his poor mother.

They filtered into school with the other children of Riverbrook, and instinctively, as is often the way, everyone seemed to realise that something was amiss, but no one said a word.

Their lessons for the day began and Johnathan sat oblivious to them all. He couldn't even have said what lesson it was, for his mind wandered far and wide over years of memories of his family, now tinted an entirely different colour.

His eyes had been opened, it seemed, to the true nature of the beast, and whether that was for better or for worse, still remained to be seen.

It was perhaps halfway through the day, during another lesson that Johnathan was paying no attention to, when something tweaked in the young boy's mind.

He didn't know exactly what it was, or why it was only then that he came to realise it, but it was much less of an idea and much more of an inclination, and one that he simply couldn't ignore at that.

Midway through the lesson, acting apparently on sheer impulse rather than anything else, for his body seemed to move without command, Johnathan simply got up and left.

Miss Falcon and his peers alike were so stunned by his sudden departure that they didn't even say anything as he rose to his feet and made for the door. His teacher's eyes followed him, but her words failed her for a few moments before she eventually found her tongue.

"Johnathan…?" She started, shocked, but he was already at the door and on his way out.

She followed him and caught the door before it closed behind him, her eyes hardening.

"Johnathan!" She demanded, more firmly this time, following him out into the corridor. "Johnathan! What do you think you're…!?" Her words trailed off as she stared after him as he walked away down the corridor.

The determination and the presence radiating all about him had never been so strong, and even Miss Falcon could feel it, and as she looked on after him as he exited the building, she simply let him walk away.

She wasn't sure exactly why she didn't stop him. She only knew that something was terribly wrong, and she sent immediately for Father Peter.

The world seemed eerily silent all about him as Johnathan walked back towards the house he called home. His pace was not slow, but then nor was it rushed. If anything, it was the measured stride of someone moving with purpose, with intent. Though, he knew not entirely what that intent was.

After an immeasurable amount of time, Johnathan walked in the front door and closed it gently behind him. He glanced briefly around and found his mother sat in the kitchen, exactly where she had been first thing that morning. Her arms were folded on the table and her head was rested upon them.

She slept fitfully and had awoken a dozen times and more since Maddie and Johnathan had left, only to doze back off again, drained and exhausted. How exactly Johnathan knew all of this, he didn't know, but nonetheless he left her be and ascended the stairs up towards his room.

The stairs creaked slightly as he climbed, but he moved swiftly and within seemingly moments found himself stood before the mirror in his bedroom.

He did not need to wait or look away. His father was already there, waiting for him.

Up until this point, Johnathan had not known who the man he saw in his reflection was. It was only now that Father Peter had told him about Arthur Knight, his true father, that the resemblance and the similarities made sense.

Still, the whole idea seemed insane.

How could he be seeing his dead father in his bedroom mirror?

But then, saying that, it wasn't the strangest thing to happen of late, Johnathan thought, and he let it go, as young minds are often inclined to do.

"Are you?" Johnathan breathed, his breath fogging the mirror slightly as he spoke, for he found now that his face was so close to it that he was mere inches from his father's reflection.

The man in his reflection only smiled and nodded at Johnathan's final realisation, and perhaps at least part of the deep void that Johnathan felt within him was slightly filled, even if only a tiny, remote corner.

That night, as Johnathan and Maddie and their mother sat around the table eating dinner, silence hung still, and they were all exhausted.

It was late, later than the time Richard would usually return home from work, and in their anxious silence they all clung to the same hopeful thought.

Finally, as dusk crept over the terrified household, it was Maddie who eventually voiced what they were all thinking.

"Maybe he isn't coming home…?" The tiny young girl half asked and half suggested, her voice admittedly a little shaky.

Emily looked across at her and smiled as best she could. Maddie immediately went to her mother and they folded into an embrace, each of them taking comfort in the other.

"Everything will be alright." Emily assured her, though the words were perhaps also to try to reassure herself. "Don't worry. It will all be just fine…"

The night crept gradually in over them, and still Richard had not returned.

At one point their front door was knocked and they all practically jumped out of their skin, but when Johnathan went to open it, he found not Richard, but instead Father Peter, and they all breathed a huge sigh of relief.

The Vicar told them that Miss Falcon had raised concerns with him when Johnathan had abruptly left school that day.

Johnathan apologised, as he knew he should, but they did not question him further, for they all knew the reason for his actions. Or, at least, they thought they did.

The old man's presence comforted them greatly, and it put them all slightly more at ease to have somebody to talk to, even if only a little, and having him there helped at least to break the dreadful silence that had seemingly been bestowed upon the household.

Eventually though, Father Peter bid them farewell for the night, assuring them that if they needed him, he would be at their beckoned call.

They thanked him of course, but fearfully, for once he was gone, they locked their doors and crept once more silently into bed. Emily and Maddie slept in together, for they were both afraid, though of course their mother would never admit that to them, for she was doing her best to reassure them.

Johnathan too was afraid, but he slept with his father in his room, just as Maddie slept in with their mother, so none of them were truly alone, but of course, he said nothing of that either.

We all have our little secrets.

Thankfully, for all three of them, sleep came a little more easily that night, though that was likely through sheer exhaustion more than anything else, and at some point during those dark hours Arthur left his son be to sleep, and Emily carried Maddie back through into her own room.

It was sleep that they all needed, and surely they would all feel better for it by the morning.

Their rest was interrupted during the darker, colder hours of the night however, and it was Johnathan who was first to rouse, in the very early hours of the morning.

His head was groggy and at first he still couldn't tell whether he was dreaming or not. His eyes were bleary and he felt an uncomfortable tingling at the back of his throat. He could smell something strange too, though he couldn't quite place it.

Beginning to cough, he pushed himself up to sit and rubbed his heavy eyes. But as he did so his coughing only worsened, and he began to splutter terribly. Glancing up quickly, the young boy's eyes widened as the smell suddenly registered in his mind, and he saw the thick, black smoke billowing in under his bedroom door.

Chapter Eleven

The skies were surprisingly clear, and Father Peter breathed in the dark air deeply, allowing it to fill his lungs completely. It was cold and it swarmed through his grateful chest eagerly, as so often the chill does.

High above him a thousand and more suns gazed down upon the solitary Vicar. He was a man of God, truly, there was no doubt about that. But nonetheless he hoped, and rather fervently at that, that one of those stars was not just the memory of Arthur Knight looking down, but in fact the still living soul of him. And perhaps, just perhaps, he could still be looking out for his family even now, from beyond the grave.

It was cold enough now that as he sighed his warm breath billowed out in front of his eyes in great steaming clouds, and those thoughts remained stuck in his head for quite some time.

He stayed there for a while, allowing the cold to seep its way into his bones, allowing his mind to wander, content with his thoughts, and allowing his heart to hope.

After half an hour or so though, his thoughts became distracted, and he took to glancing around frequently, almost even agitatedly.

It was most likely the cold, he surmised, pulling his thick cloak around his shoulders a little tighter, though it did very little to ward off the chill he had already allowed to invade his body.

As he finally moved off, his legs stiff from standing still, a strange crackling and popping sound caught his attention.

Looking around however, he saw nothing that betrayed the sound.

Emily's house was still in view, as were several others, and he could even make out the outline of the spire of the church in the distance, by the dim light of the stars.

Continuing, he shrugged off the sound as it died and faded away and he could no longer hear it. Perhaps he was simply tired and his mind was playing tricks on him. He had lost a lot of sleep recently, worrying for Emily and her family no less.

Suddenly a bright orange flash illuminated the night, and the gentle popping and crackling roared into new life and bellowed with ferocity to match the blinding light.

Father Peter gasped, startled, and spun around to face the light, though at first he could not see and had to shield his eyes from the orange glare.

Then the heat hit him, and with it dawned the terrible truth.

He felt as if his heart was in his mouth.

It couldn't be.

"EMILY!!" He yelled suddenly, shock and fear gripping him as he bolted forwards towards the fierce blaze that now engulfed the cottage, still with Emily and Maddie and Johnathan inside.

The flames swelled and rose, spreading so quickly that before he was even within two dozen feet of the fire, it had swallowed the house entirely, blocking his every entry and, even worse, blocking their every escape.

For more times than he cared to count, the old Vicar tried to fight his way through the dancing flames. But even as they toyed with him and appeared to open up a safe passage, the second he tried to pass they instantly closed ranks and licked at him menacingly, spitting at his clothes and exposed skin with their spiteful tongues.

More than once he found himself singed and his robes burned, before eventually, after many failed attempts, he knew he would not be able to force his way in.

There were others there now too. Shouts and cries of dismay and horror mixed with those of action as some people scrambled for buckets of water and sand. But the old man knew it was far too late for that. The flames engulfed every part of the house now, and it would be an absolute miracle if anybody was still alive.

He was a devout man, but if anybody in the world believed in miracles, he certainly did.

All of a sudden he saw movement from inside the house, through an open upstairs window. His heart swelled and rejoiced for a moment, before sinking again as yet even more flames swelled into the frame.

The flames were everywhere.

He was just giving himself false hope.

But no, once again the flickering flames in the window died down slightly and he saw the same glimpse of movement, different to the blinding tongues of fire all around.

Voices in the Mirror

He was no longer cold, and the chill in his muscles had certainly faded, through the intense heat from the blaze and through fear and adrenaline both.

But then, amidst the blinding oranges and reds and yellows awash before him, the old Vicar saw something more clearly through the window. Silhouetted against the blinding flashes and starts that overwhelmed the house, he could just about make out a single, lonely shape.

This single figure, even in that briefest of glances, he recognised, and a lump caught in his throat and his eyes widened. Perhaps it was fear that gripped him, or shock maybe, or perhaps simply he was dumfounded, he didn't really know.

But regardless, he was absolutely certain of what he saw.

"Arthur…?" He whispered, though to whom he was speaking it mattered not. The words simply escaped his lips of their own free will.

Of course, whomever it was he saw amidst the blazing inferno, they did not hear him: there was simply no way they could have done. The flames roared and bellowed furiously, by now drowning out the sound of all else.

Other cries for help were lost to the sound, overshadowed by it completely, and still nobody could do a thing to stop the blazing inferno.

Then the figure in the window vanished, overwhelmed like everything else by the searing flames. Father Peter took an automatic and involuntary step forward, but he was forced back by the intense lash of the heat as it threatened to scald him.

One side of the roof then, thatched just the same as all the others, reached its limit, collapsing into its stone foundations, disintegrating and practically pouring into the house below like molten rock.

Suddenly a silhouette flashed in and out of view through the boiling, shimmering air, recoiling briefly in the arch to the front door as the flames attacked relentlessly.

The figure vanished once again and the old man's heart sank, beginning to truly believe now that he was just seeing things, and that in fact the three of them: Emily and Maddie and Johnathan, were all already dead.

But he was wrong.

All of a sudden the silhouette reappeared, standing tall now, and a man burst from the flames cradling a young girl tenderly in his arms.

The old Vicar's eyes widened.

He had been right.

It was Arthur.

He was exactly as Father Peter remembered him: tall, broad, strong, brave. His face was black, his chest heaved, and his arms and legs were badly burned.

Arthur looked gravely at the old man for a brief moment, before laying Maddie gently down upon the ground and vanishing back into the scorching flames yet again, ignoring all of the pain he was enduring.

Within mere moments, before Father Peter even had a chance to catch his breath, Arthur reappeared, this time clasping Emily protectively in his arms. He carried his wife as if she weighed nothing, and though she had suffered only a few minor burns, she clung desperately to him, seeming to never want to let go.

He carried her over and carefully set her down on the floor beside Maddie.

The old man could only watch in awe as Arthur stooped to one knee and laid his wife safely next to their daughter.

And there he stayed for a moment, bowing his head slightly in relief, resting his hand tenderly upon the back of his wife's head, holding her even still.

Then he leaned forward and kissed Emily on her forehead, and then Maddie too, before sighing deeply and rising to his feet to face Father Peter.

The Vicar gasped as Arthur rose to his feet, for as the old man's eyes flickered to his face, it was not Arthur that they found, but instead Johnathan. He blinked a few times disbelievingly, but no, it was Johnathan who stood protectively over Emily and Maddie, his mother and sister.

But then, as if a great dam had been released and all of his strength had been entirely drained from him, Johnathan shuddered terribly and his legs buckled beneath him.

He collapsed heavily to the floor, crumpling to the ground, ruined.

Chapter Twelve

Johnathan leapt from his bed, fear instantly gripping his heart. He darted immediately for his bedroom door and reached out his hand to open it.

But then he froze for a moment, not knowing whether he should or not. Wouldn't it just make the fire worse?

It was too late now. He had no choice.

Gritting his teeth, he yanked the door open and leapt back with a cry as the flames exploded through the doorway towards him.

He cursed loudly and took a few tentative steps back, his mind racing and his lungs filling with smoke, only making him cough and splutter evermore heavily.

Suddenly, as he stepped back, he caught a glimpse of his reflection in his mirror, and saw his father staring back as him, angst strewn across his face.

"What do I do!?" Johnathan yelled desperately at his reflection, waving his arms in panic, terrified.

Arthur did not reply. Whether he didn't, or couldn't, Johnathan wasn't sure, but instead his reflection of his father reached out his hand, and Johnathan felt himself doing the same, even despite the circumstances.

The second Johnathan fingertips touched the mirror, at exactly the same point that his father's reached forward, endless amounts of time suddenly passed between them.

In that moment, Johnathan saw the whole world through not his own eyes, but instead through his father's.

Everything his father had ever learned and taught and heard and tasted and smelled and felt. Every emotion, every love, every anger, every lesson, all passed from father to son in that single instant.

And suddenly Johnathan was painfully aware that, even if he did survive this fire, the fight would never end.

No matter what happened, it would never be over.

Johnathan felt a surge race through his body, as if he had all of a sudden been reinvigorated. It was as if the veil had once again descended upon him, but instead this time instead of engulfing him, it was coming from deep within.

Then, within seconds, Johnathan snapped his eyes forwards and back to the doorway. Instantly he made his decision.

He knew he had very little time, but indeed also that he had even less choice.

Surging forwards Johnathan charged and leapt through the angry flames. He felt their orange tongues lick at his legs and scald and mottle his skin, but he gritted his teeth and set his jaw against the searing pain.

He darted left and right, avoiding the worst of the blazes as best as he could, but some suffering was inevitable, as is all too often the way.

The young boy's lungs heaved and he tried desperately not to inhale too much of the smoke. But no matter how much experience he had just gleaned, he was still only, fatally, human.

Seeing that Maddie's bedroom door was still closed Johnathan darted to the left and then used his momentum to launch himself directly at her door. He crashed through the wooden barricade, exploding into his sister's bedroom with a sudden burst and swell of flames.

Maddie screamed in fear as her brother erupted into her room.

Johnathan rolled like a cat and found his feet, burned and painful as they were, and went immediately to his sister, huddled in the corner of her room, terrified and alone.

"Maddie!" He exclaimed, though the sound came out in a rasping cough and heave and wheeze, as his lungs struggled desperately for air.

"Johnathan?" His sister wheezed in return, looking up at him through streaming eyes.

"We need to go!" He managed then, scooping her into his arms and rising to his feet.

Maddie looked confused and stared at Johnathan's face with a mixture of relief and disbelief, but she said no more and simply allowed him to carry her back over to her bed. He wrapped his sister's blanket around her and turned yet again to face the flames.

"MADDIE!! JOHNATHAN!!" Their mother screamed desperately through the encroaching flames, coughing and gagging as she yelled, barely able to breathe.

Her bedroom door was still in pieces and already the flames were in her room, reaching out for her with their cruel fingers and tendrils, desperate to mark her with their fatal kiss.

Then, seemingly from the very heart of the flames, the impossible happened.

"Arthur…?" Emily gasped on heaving lungs as her husband appeared through the deadly fire, carrying their daughter wrapped in a blanket.

Her legs buckled beneath her.

She must have been hallucinating.

She must have been dying.

But she wasn't.

Arthur knelt down beside her and put his hand upon her arm.

"There's no time. We have to go." His voice told her, his tone deadly serious. But it was not her husband's voice that spoke to her, it was her son's.

Emily looked down at the hand upon her arm and reached for it, grasping it tightly.

It was definitely there; she wasn't going crazy.

Looking back up then, she saw that in fact it wasn't her husband, it was her son, Johnathan, carrying Maddie, and his hand that was outstretched holding hers.

"We need to go." He repeated, urging her to her feet.

Emily nodded dumbly, confused and afraid, and scrambled to her feet, though they both stooped in an almost futile attempt to keep out of the worst of the smoke.

Johnathan turned to the doorway and, though she just shrugged it off and blamed her fear for it, Emily could have sworn that she saw her son's figure shimmer into the size of a man in the orange light.

He seemed to be waiting for a break in the flames, but a minute or so later the smoke hanging in the bedroom was almost unbearable, and no such opportunity had reared its head.

Cursing loudly, Johnathan shifted Maddie onto one arm and without even pausing to ask, scooped his mother, Emily, up into his other arm, carrying them both on his young frame as if they barely weighed anything at all.

Without a thought then, his heart racing and thumping against his chest, Johnathan plunged back onto the landing. Immediately the flames singed his already burned legs and sent searing pain through him anew.

But, as before, there was nothing that could be done, and he just gritted his teeth and ignored it, taking to the stairs immediately. He whispered a silent prayer that they were not too badly damaged by the flames that they wouldn't hold the weight of the three of them.

Luckily they held, just about, but even as he reached the last few steps, he realised suddenly that the staircase wasn't the biggest problem.

Even as the fires ravaged and roared and screamed all about him, he heard a huge groaning and cracking above him, and realised all of a sudden that the roof was coming down, and it wasn't going to wait for them to get out.

He cursed foully again and practically dove across the dining room to throw Maddie and Emily beneath the table in the kitchen, and he reached it not a moment too soon, for even as he did, the ceiling thundered down on top of him, pouring molten thatch and timber upon his head.

Raising his arms to protect himself, the full weight of the roof bore down upon the young boy, and the impact drove him to his knees. He grunted loudly as the full force of it threw itself at him.

"JOHNATHAN!" Maddie screamed, trying to scramble out from under the table to help him, but Emily held her back.

"NO!" Johnathan barked, even as the scalding ceiling seared his arms and threatened to crush him entirely. "Stay there!"

Emily screamed then, though she still refused to leg Maddie go, as the flames spread and licked at her legs beneath the table, for the fallen ceiling had set it to the burn yet even faster.

The sound of her suffering seemed to give Johnathan renewed strength, and with a great, roaring cry he exploded to his feet and threw the massive fallen timbers and melted thatch across the room, shifting them with apparent inhuman strength.

Immediately he reached under the table and dragged his petrified sister out and onto his arm once more. He reached back for Emily too, but she pushed out against him, seeing how hurt he already was.

"Just go!" She shouted to him. "I'll follow you!"

There was no time to argue. Johnathan nodded once and turned for the door, darting immediately forwards.

Emily scrambled to follow, but no matter how hard she tried, she could not move as fast as her son.

It was as though he was instilled with a strength that belonged to another.

She had only ever known one person with that kind of strength, and he had been killed a long time ago.

Johnathan reached the doorway and recoiled for a moment as the flames reared in his face, threatening to engulf him completely, but then they dulled slightly and he saw his chance, surging forward with all the speed he could muster.

Finally, after what felt like an eternity, he broke out into the cool, dark of the night beneath a star-spattered sky.

The relief was instant and unbelievable and his lungs filled with cool, clean air.

There was no time to revel however. He glanced up briefly and laid eyes instantly upon Father Peter. The old man looked shocked beyond all description. Johnathan said nothing however, and simply laid his sister gently down upon the floor before turning on his heel and plunging directly back into the flames, for Emily had not managed to follow him out.

Fear struck at his heart as he re-entered the house and couldn't immediately see her. Strength flushed through him anew for some reason and he raced back through into the kitchen, his body seeming to move automatically.

Even as he swam through the inferno all around, the heat hit him once again, like a brick wall, and his body threatened to give in to the onslaught.

And then there she was, cowering from the overwhelming flames and heat and smog, coughing and spluttering, unable to move.

Without thinking he swept her into his arms and lurched back towards the door.

His lungs burned for air, his legs and arms just burned, and his body screamed at him for relief.

But all of this Johnathan ignored. He had to get them both out. He had to save his family.

Even in that brief moment, strangely, amidst all the panic and fear, he realised that that desperate, driving wish wasn't simply his own, and that there was another set of thoughts merged with his, willing and wishing and urging for exactly the same thing.

Suddenly the cool night's air hit him once again and he was free of the blazing firestorm, and the respite that washed over him was exulting.

He darted straight back to Maddie's side and laid his mother down next to his sister, sinking to his knees as he did so, utterly exhausted.

As he placed Emily gently down upon the cold grass, his hand stayed upon her head and he looked at them both for a moment, though he felt as though he wasn't seeing them through his own eyes.

He leant forward and kissed them each in turn on their foreheads, before sighing, rising slowly to his feet and, once again, laying his level gaze upon the old Vicar stood before him.

The young boy winced suddenly as the adrenaline that had rushed and surged through his veins dumped completely.

His strength failed him within a moment and his body seared to life with fresh pain of his injuries, and he promptly collapsed to the floor, his body shuddering and crumbling to a desecrated heap.

Chapter Thirteen

Father Peter rushed over to the three of them, lay coughing and spluttering on the cool grass beneath the light spattered blanket hanging high above them.

His eyes flitted across their steaming bodies.

Maddie, though partly wrapped still in a blanket, seemed to be ok besides her heaving chest. Emily and Johnathan both had quite severe burns, she on her legs, and he across seemingly his whole body.

Soon others swarmed round them too, and gasps became immediately evident.

"Are they okay!?" Someone asked, though surely the scene that lay before them should have answered that question.

"What happened!?" Someone else demanded then, looking fervently between the three on the floor and the collapsed, flaming house, though that question too seemed to have an obvious answer.

But Father Peter had another question in mind, and didn't need that particular one answering.

He knew exactly who was responsible for this, and for the first time in a long time, anger flowed afresh through his veins.

Then he took control.

"Bring them to the church!" He instructed, talking to no one in particular, but his tone had that ring of immediate finality to it that drove the men and women around him instantly into action.

"Dorian!" The old Vicar barked then, spying the shopkeeper in the darkness. "I need poultices, and dressings, and ice. Bring them to the church. Lots of them."

The man obeyed inherently and disappeared off into the darkness at a dead run.

A makeshift litter had appeared beside Maddie and Emily and Johnathan, constructed hastily of broomsticks and bedsheets. Regardless, it would do the job.

"Let's go!" The old man instructed, heading off immediately for the church, with his villagers and patients in tow, not wasting a moment more.

It was many hours later, deep into the night and even further into morning that Father Peter cared for his patients, his dear friends. He worked relentlessly to treat and dress their wounds. Some of their burns he realised, especially Johnathan's, were extensive and very severe, and they required an awful lot of attention.

He had a few other willing volunteers with him also to help him attend to them, so all three could receive treatment at once. The team worked ceaselessly and the darkness wore on as they mixed herbs and ointments and applied ice and dressings carefully and anxiously, their movements illuminated only, and rather ironically, by flickering candlelight.

Finally, though they were still not conscious, by the early hours of the morning, not far off sunrise, Maddie, Emily and Johnathan's breathing was at least a little stronger, and their wounds were dressed. They would need to be changed again soon, but for now in any case, there was no more anybody could do.

Father Peter thanked those who had stayed to help him, and even as they left, others streamed in to see how the Davies were doing.

How little they knew.

This parade of visitors continued for quite some time, marching in and out of the church to stand by the beds upon which the Davies family lay. The beds had been brought in from a nearby cottage and sat in a room off to the side of the main hall.

After a full morning and afternoon of streaming visits, Father Peter eventually closed the doors to the vast church, sealing Emily and Maddie and Johnathan safely inside, knowing they needed peace and quiet and rest.

It was perhaps only an hour or so after that when Emily and her daughter began to stir, wheezing and coughing and spluttering as they awoke.

The sky was a gradually darkening purple above the tall spire of Riverbrook's church, and thin wisps of cloud spread long and wide in dark billowed rows across its vast expansive face. A chill breeze wound its way over the hills and through the trees and across the icy cold river that cut through the very beating heart of the village, striking its biting chill at the very centre of the place Emily had for a long time called home.

She awoke with a start, jerking up to sit with a gasp. But that immediately turned into a coughing fit that tore painfully at her damaged throat and lungs. She groaned and clutched at her chest, clenching her fists as if to fight away the pain. But it did not cease.

The sound woke Maddie also, and she went through an identical ritual before managing to eventually catch her breath too.

Emily hissed then as she twisted on the bedsheets and her legs burned with fresh pain. She clenched her teeth and made an automatic growling noise at the back of her throat, only to be rewarded with a fresh coughing fit, pulling at her chest once again.

"How are you feeling?" A voice asked gently, and between splutters Emily and Maddie saw Father Peter enter the room across from their beds, having heard them struggling presumably.

The room was dim and Emily could only just about make out the Vicar's face by the lantern he carried.

"Awful." Emily managed between fits. Then she looked across at Maddie.

"Y…Yeah…" Her daughter managed between fits also. "Awful."

"Johnathan!?" Emily suddenly cried, spying that her son was still asleep, her eyes slowly adjusting to the dim light. She scrambled to her feet, but cried out in pain as she tried to stand. Nonetheless though, pushing through it with gritted teeth once again, she staggered over to her son's bedside.

Her whole body hurt, and as the old man joined her at Johnathan's side, she could only imagine how he felt as the light from Father Peter's lantern revealed the extent of her son's wounds.

Emily's breath caught in her throat, and she felt Maddie shudder in horror at her side. She quickly, and painfully, lifted her daughter into her arms, pressing her head gently against her chest.

Maddie began to cry immediately, for she knew Johnathan was very badly hurt, and no matter how much her mother shielded her or tried to quiet her, her brother had endured this of his own free will, all to save them from the fire.

The little girl choked as she cried, for her throat and chest burned too, and she remembered exactly how it had felt not being able to breathe in her bedroom, and how terrified she had been watching the smoke billow in.

She shuddered again.

"He's very weak." Father Peter explained in a hushed voice, the sound of it penetrating the gloomy darkness. "His wounds are very bad."

He told them the truth, because he knew they would not believe anything else, and the last thing they needed now was lies, after all these years.

Emily nodded, knowing this also, and she reached out tentatively with one hand, still holding Maddie with the other arm.

Johnathan's legs and arms and hands and even parts of his face and shoulders were badly burned, but there was one side of his left hand that seemed to have escaped the flames, and so Emily instinctively reached for that, wanting just to be there for her son in any way that she could. In any way that she knew how.

Anything would be better than nothing.
Or so she surmised at least.

The evening drew on and the purple in the sky turned slowly richer and deeper until eventually it faded completely to black, sprinkled all over with glittering stars and a moon seemingly so close and so bright that it appeared to glow amidst the darkness.

It was a perfectly round midnight sun, fighting desperately against the endless night.

It was as that same moonlight strayed hopelessly into the path of the never ending night, many hours later, when Johnathan slowly and silently stirred from his deep slumber.

He did not awake with a start or a jump as his mother and sister had done, but rather his racing mind slowly brought him back to consciousness.

His dreams were wild and filled with fire and smoke and pain, and he saw himself running endlessly through corridors and up and down stairways trying desperately to reach mother and his sister.

No matter how fast he ran though, or how high he climbed, his search seemed to be never ending, and the flames closed in around him, encircling him.

Finally, having run until he was exhausted, and climbed until his legs would drive him on no further, Johnathan came to a defeated halt.

It was then that he awoke.

His eyes slowly opened and the dreadful realisation that had dawned upon him in his dream carried through and rang true in reality too.

Even though he recalled the events of the fire, as he lay there silently in the dark, and he knew that he had managed to get them out, it wasn't over.

It wasn't the fire that wanted to harm them.

It was Richard.

Of course, there would be no proof. Johnathan didn't even need to ask that. He knew it. But at the same time, equally, he knew that Richard was responsible.

Things had gotten way out of control.

Years of distrust and hatred and anger that he hadn't even known about, were coming suddenly boiling and bubbling to the surface, and they were threatening and unchecked, running rampant through his family like a charging bull.

He had to stop it.

But what could he do?

He didn't really know.

All he knew was that he had to do something.

Chapter Fourteen

Raising slowly up off the bed and into a sitting position was an excruciating endeavour, and all the while Johnathan tried desperately not to make a sound, for he did not wish to wake his mother and sister. Though the room was too dark to see them, for the door was closed and no light crept in through the darkened window, he could hear their quiet, slow, paced breathing.

He swivelled his legs around to hang off the bed and took a few slow, deep breaths. He could feel the dressings pulling at his arms and shoulders and back and legs, and he shuddered at the thought of his injuries.

Trying not to think about it, he pushed himself off the bed and staggered slightly to keep his feet. His head spun terribly and for a moment Johnathan thought he was going to be sick. The nausea passed after a minute or two however, and he stumbled as quietly as he could across the room to where he could see the faintly flickering light of a candle from underneath the door.

Luckily the door opened without making too much noise, and the faint creaking did not stir Emily or Maddie.

Johnathan pulled the door inaudibly closed behind him and leant heavily on the wall for a moment, catching his breath.

"They'll be upset you didn't wake them, you know." Father Peter's voice sounded quietly from over on one of the pews. Johnathan looked up to see him sat very still with his hands in his lap, staring forwards in an oddly pensive manner.

His mood seemed to be a most thoughtful one.

"They need to rest." Johnathan replied by way of explanation, wincing as he hobbled over from the door to the pew where Father Peter sat.

"And you don't?" The old man questioned.

Johnathan didn't reply at first, but instead lowered himself onto the wooden bench next to the old Vicar and sighed deeply, relaxing his legs.

"I had no idea things would ever go this far…" Father Peter spoke again then, still gazing wistfully forward, as if looking for something that had eluded him for a very long time.

"It isn't your fault…" Johnathan replied automatically.

"It could have been an accident…" The old man suggested, but Johnathan gave him a withering look and he sighed deeply. "No, you're right." He agreed. "Things have gotten completely out of hand. Richard is out of his mind."

"What can we do?" The young boy asked.

"I'm not sure." Father Peter admitted honestly. "We must be careful." He warned. "Clearly all three of you are in terrible danger. Perhaps even more so now that you've escaped the fire. He won't be happy about that at all. It was a very risky thing to do anyway. If none of you had made it out, it may have been passed off as an accident, but now, he knows you'll find out the truth."

"So he'll try again?" Johnathan asked, his voice serious and dripping with undisguised malice for the man he had for so long called father.

"I fear he won't cease until either it's finished, or until someone stops him…" Father Peter replied in a voice that betrayed quite fatally his own despair at the situation.

Silence fell over the two of them then for some time, and yet still it was too early for the sun to creep its head over the horizon. The only light came from the dancing candles. So relaxing to watch, Johnathan mused, but then, as he tried to shift his weight slightly and grimaced, he was reminded of exactly how much pain such a beautiful thing can cause.

"Father Peter…" Johnathan started then, his voice hesitant, and the old Vicar looked over at the young boy Johnathan with tired, yet curious, eyes.

"Yes…?" He asked, sensing the shift in Johnathan's tone, wondering what was on his mind.

As of late the troubled Vicar had come to miss the old days when Emily had brought Johnathan and Maddie to see him simply out of care. She had often come by way of thanks too, he had always thought.

That seemed wildly inappropriate now though, considering the circumstances. Recently the old Vicar had begun to think that perhaps he had made a mistake by not intervening.

But then, what choice had he had.

Everybody is entitled to live their own lives.

Everybody must live their own lives, and make their own choices, and indeed mistakes, regardless of what happens.

"What was my father like?" He asked then. "I know you've told the stories about Riverbrook…" Johnathan added then. "But what was he really like? As a person?"

"What was Arthur really like?" The old man repeated, musing aloud, his hand coming to his silvery whiskered chin automatically.

Johnathan watched the old man as he recalled memories of Arthur, and wished suddenly that he too could remember his father. He didn't want second hand accounts of him, really, he wanted to be able to remember him for himself.

"He was a very good man, Johnathan." The old man began slowly. "He was a great man in fact."

"Why?" The young boy asked.

"There are two main things that I remember about your father, above all else…" The Vicar mused aloud then, in response to Johnathan's query. "I remember that he loved your mother. He loved her very much."

Johnathan nodded, smiling faintly, pleased by that, but equally reminded of Richard and all the pain he had brought Johnathan's family, even without them knowing.

"And secondly…" The old man continued. "I remember that Arthur could do anything, for anybody…"

The young boy's brow furrowed then and his expression asked the question on his tongue without even needing to speak.

"It was the same for as long as I knew him…" The old Vicar continued, as if that explained everything. "Riverbrook needed a leader, a figurehead: he took on the responsibility without second thought. The village needed a school: he built one. When he needed to be a father and a husband, he was wonderful. Your mother adored him so…"

"I'm sure she still does…" Johnathan replied then, recalling the desperate hope in her mother's eyes when she had mistaken him for his father, both when Johnathan had stopped Richard from beating her, and then also when Johnathan had saved her from the flames that Richard had set to consume her.

"Of that I have no doubt." Father Peter agreed. "It was not the sort of bond to be so easily forgotten.

Johnathan sighed then. So many things had happened. And not just recently, but over the years, he imagined, there were so many things that he didn't even know about.

"Try not to dwell on it too much, Johnathan." Father Peter advised gently. "I know things are not at their best, but none of it's your doing. You've done nothing but good." He laughed shortly then at his own words. "Funnily enough, you remind me of your father. He would be very proud of you."

Johnathan smiled at that, for strangely enough he found much comfort in that particular comment, as if for years that was all he'd ever really wanted to hear.

Father Peter could see the impact of what he'd said, and he smiled reassuringly. Then, after a few more moments, his expression became more serious, and he spoke again to the young boy.

"Johnathan…" He began, his tone dropping slightly. "Have you been speaking to your father?" He asked. "Is there a way you contact him?"

Of course, at face value, what the old Vicar was asking was absurd. He was asking a twelve-year-old boy if he could communicate with the dead. Yet, in all his life, he had never asked a question of anybody with so much hope hanging on his words.

He had always in years gone by been able to turn to Arthur Knight, safe in the knowledge that he, above all others, would know exactly what to do. And now, seemingly, even after all these years, even though Arthur was dead, here the old Vicar was, crazily still hoping for the same thing.

Johnathan struggled for words for a minute or so, and the Vicar awaited his response, perhaps inwardly not quite as patiently as he should have done, but he did his best not to let it show.

"It's complicated." Johnathan finally admitted, sighing heavily. "He's not always there, and I'm sure sometimes he's there and I don't even know it…"

"When is he there?" Father Peter asked.

Johnathan thought for a moment more, considering that.

"Whenever I need him." Johnathan admitted again, though this time a slight smile touched his lips.

He hadn't thought of it in that way before.

"So, when you need him…" The old man continued, considering carefully the way he phrased his question. "How do you speak to him…? How does he come to you…?"

The young boy looked up for a moment. The answer to that one was much easier, but made him sound no less insane, certainly. He felt he could tell Father Peter though. If there was anybody in the world he could tell that wasn't his sister, it would have been the old Vicar.

Johnathan sighed.

"It's gone now…" He started. "After the fire…There was an old mirror in my bedroom. It used to belong to my grandfather…"

The Vicar's face was awash with intrigue and sudden understanding, but there still lingered traces of slight confusion in his expression.

"So can't you speak to him now?" The old man asked, unsure exactly what Johnathan was trying to say.

"I don't know…" He confessed, sighing yet again.

The old man smiled reassuringly.

"Don't worry." He said then, placing his hand on the back of Johnathan's hand, the only part of him that wasn't bandaged. "Arthur will find a way, and if he can't, I know you will."

The young boy looked at Father Peter then with eyes full of curiosity and intrigue. The old Vicar seemed to have more faith in him than he did in himself. Though somehow he perceived that was usually the way, and indeed the reason why anybody ever failed at anything in the first place.

Seeing Johnathan's realisation, Father Peter smiled. On first thought, what he was asking of Johnathan seemed to be impossible, insane, and ridiculous even.

But of late, the line that he had believed lay between the possible and the impossible, had become somewhat blurred and twisted, until now he wasn't entirely sure if it even still existed.

The young boy sat before him processed what the Vicar had asked of him, and Father Peter watched in awe as Johnathan's expression flickered through emotions like water skims over rock.

First he looked confused and lost, then he set deep into thought and concentration, and finally that thoughtful gaze was eventually replaced by a determination painted so obviously across Johnathan's face that it may as well have been Arthur sitting before him.

Like father, like son.

That look told Father Peter then that, if this young Knight had anything to do with it, nothing was impossible.

Suddenly, light flooded the hall as the sun broke the horizon, far off to the east, and its golden rays were warm and comforting upon Johnathan's face as they streamed in through the stained glass windows set high above.

Johnathan looked up and examined the varying scenes that the shining windows depicted.

One showed an angel, hovering up above the clouds looking down upon the masses far below him with a look of sorrow and regret pained across his face. His hands looked as though they had fallen to his sides in defeat and his head bowed mournfully.

Another portrayed a great, powerful knight, clad in full armour, bearing a heavy shield that was shaped like a massive kite, and a broadsword so large that the young boy wondered how he would even have been able to lift it. Nonetheless, the knight was doing battle with a fierce beast of some kind, with fangs that searched hungrily for flesh and eyes that bore into the hero like knives.

Each coloured glass window told a different story, undoubtedly each of which could be interpreted in a thousand different ways and more.

Johnathan sighed as he glanced all around, feeling decidedly melancholy all of a sudden.

But then, as if exactly on cue, the door to the room that Johnathan had awoken in creaked slowly open, and out emerged his mother, Emily, and his dear little sister, Maddie.

"Johnathan!" Maddie cried, springing towards him, and Emily's face was awash with great relief.

Resisting the urge right at the last moment, Maddie stopped herself short just before she threw herself on her brother to hug him. She eyed his dressings warily and even looked a little sheepish.

"How are you feeling?" She asked then, her voice a little timid, as if she had been shot down.

"Oh, Maddie." Johnathan said then, laughing slightly. He climbed immediately to his feet, hiding his pain, and pulled her up into his arms. She hugged him back gratefully and he winced inwardly, but he didn't care. It was far more than worth it.

Emily crossed over the pews then to him too, restraining herself from leaping with relief, though only just.

"My Johnathan…" She said quietly, her voice almost a whisper as she clasped him gently into her arms.

Holding him for a moment, suddenly everything felt like it would all be alright again.

"What were you thinking?" She asked him then. Her tone not accusing, only concerned, and he looked back at his mother's liquid blue eyes very seriously.

"I had to get you out." He replied simply, looking slowly between Emily and Maddie, with not a hint of anything but love in his voice.

They simply stared back at Johnathan, knowing not what they could say. There was no way they could reprimand him. They were only upset because his actions had very nearly cost them the ultimate price.

Before either of them could respond, however, Johnathan's expression shifted and turned back solely to his mother. Her heart fluttered and guilt surged through her veins, whether it was misplaced or not, she didn't know.

She did, however, know exactly what he was going to ask, even before he drew breath to speak.

His expression said a thousand times more than the question forming in his mind ever could.

A single tear escaped her and streamed down her hot, flushed cheek, as her son's eyes looked right into her very soul, into the core of her being: the very place where she hid all of her guilt and mourning and suffering, housed there, purposefully, forevermore, until the day she would eventually die and it would all be forgotten.

"I'm sorry…" Emily Knight breathed, flooding the nave suddenly with her sorrow and her grief, for they had been simmering for years, and their effect was sudden and frightful.

Chapter Fifteen

How did this happen?

Why did it happen?

How hadn't he known?

Why hadn't she put a stop to it!?

No one in the village would had stood for it! Richard would have been thrown out!

How in God's name had he been allowed to get away with this for so long!?

A thousand and more questions flooded through Johnathan's mind, and he had absolutely no way of determining which to ask, how he would ask them, or if they were even relevant.

Finally, after staring at his mother's stricken face for almost longer than he could bear, he settled for the simplest request of all.

"Tell me." He said quietly, his voice level and serious and far beyond that of a mere twelve-year-old.

Although, that was quite possibly because it wasn't just him who was speaking, but at that point, that matter definitely wasn't relevant.

"Tell me everything."

Emily took a deep, quivering breath and glanced briefly at Father Peter, almost as if for reassurance. The old man smiled and nodded encouragingly at her. She pursed her lips and looked back to her awaiting children.

Johnathan sat upon the pews again, for standing drained his strength, and Maddie perched close by his side, her hand in his, keeping her safe.

"Alright…" Emily eventually said, exhaling deeply and summing as much courage as she could muster.

For all these years, hiding the truth had been hard, but it had become second nature to her. She had bottled up everything and shoved it down deep inside of her. Now, faced with revealing it all and exposing her every fragile nerve, she felt more afraid than ever before, and Emily's grief threatened to overwhelm her completely as it washed over her and raced through her heart and her veins in great flooding waves.

"Your real father's name is Arthur, Arthur Knight."

Johnathan felt Maddie stir immediately and her little hand in his own tightened. He quieted her gently and pulled her even closer, enveloping his baby sister into his arms, holding her close, protecting her as always.

"I came to Riverbrook many years ago, almost fifteen now." Emily began, and her voice cracked with rushing emotion as all her supressed memories came flooding back to her. "I don't know what brought me here. All of a sudden I just felt an overwhelming desire to leave home."

Father Peter's expression was one of understanding and compassion, whilst Maddie was still struggling to keep herself from bursting into tears, and Johnathan's face was entirely unreadable.

"I lived in the far south." His mother continued. "Right by the coast. I was happy. But out of nowhere, I just up and left home. I came north, not really following any path or track in particular…"

Emily told her children of how her random wanderings had taken her far and wide, and though during that time she didn't know what it was exactly she was looking for, in every place that she found herself, she knew inherently that she had not yet discovered it.

She told them of all the places she visited and the people she met and the wonders she saw, and that yet even still none of it had ever seemed enough.

Some of the sights that she had beheld in that time, some of the people she had grown to know and love, some of the things she had experienced, had been truly extraordinary.

Nonetheless, every time, she had always somehow subconsciously decided that this wasn't what she was searching for, and had moved on, forever on the move, never settling in one place or another for more than a few weeks, or at the most months.

"And then eventually I reached a river. It ran west to east, blocking my way north."

"Did you cross it?" Johnathan asked then, though not really knowing why that question had been so necessary for him to ask.

"No." His mother admitted, smiling fondly at the memory as it flitted through her mind. "I decided to follow it west, and in the end the river started to wind its way north anyway, but I didn't follow it all the way…"

"Why not?" Maddie asked then, piping up for the first time in quite some time.

"Because I found what I was looking for." Her mother replied immediately, as if there was no possible other explanation.

"What did you find?" The young girl asked then, looking up almost longingly at her mother, as if this explanation was all she had ever wanted to hear.

"I found Riverbrook, or the beginnings of it anyway." She replied simply. "But, more importantly, I found your father."

With great energy and enthusiasm then, Emily Knight began to describe to her children the world she had accidentally, or perhaps by way of fate, she would never know, stumbled in to.

Her explanations were detailed, eloquent and elegant, as if she had been there only yesterday.

Her recollections of Arthur Knight, the first time she had met him, and indeed also seemingly every occasion following that too, were vivid and clear down to every last details, and she wove great descriptions of what he had said, how he had said it, and even the expressions on his face as he had talked.

Clearly she had loved him immediately, and completely. Aside from all else, those truths were plain to see.

And even as Emily's memories spread to the rest of the village and its progress, always she came back to one thing: her dear Arthur Knight.

"I fell in love with him…" She continued then, though by that point there was no way either Maddie or Johnathan could possibly have missed that fact. "Soon we were wed and I fell pregnant with you, Johnathan…"

"What happened then?" Her young son asked, but even as he spoke, he knew what was would soon come, and he began to feel physically sick to his stomach.

"In time you were born. We lived in the cottage. We were very happy."

Emily's eyes at that point brimmed with so many memories that she was almost on the verge of tears.

"I fell pregnant again, and soon enough Maddie was born…" She recalled, though at that point her voice began to trail off, for she knew what the next part to this beautiful tale was.

So did Johnathan, and the pain he felt stabbing at his chest in that moment was like nothing he had ever experienced. It was a knife jabbing at his heart that twisted cruelly between his ribs and flushed his lungs with panic.

Somehow, instinctively, he knew that the pain he felt was not entirely his own, but that his father was also hearing Emily's words, and they stung at him with such fierce intensity that the agony was almost unbearable.

"Then it happened." Johnathan's mother stated ominously, as if those three words said all that needed to be heard.

And indeed they were not the traditional three words that mean so much more than they seem to say.

"What happened?" Johnathan asked. His voice was icy cold and he could feel Maddie trembling as she pressed even closer to him.

"Arthur didn't come home one day." Emily said, taking quick, shallow breaths, as if somehow believing the less air she breathed in the less painful the words would be. "It was two days before his body was found…"

A sob escaped Emily then and her barricades crumbled and tears began to stream openly down her cheeks. Innately, Maddie too burst into tears and ran to her mother, who swept her up in a fierce embrace. Again, though it was irrational, it was almost as if she believed that the more love she gave her children, the more it would make up for the love she wanted so desperately to devote to her husband.

She went on then to tell them how Arthur's body had been found by the river. She explained to them how it had looked like he'd been mugged and killed, and everyone mourned his passing.

But none had grieved so much as their mother, Maddie and Johnathan gathered, and even as she spoke and her voice wavered, broken and disjointed by devastated sobs, still now they could tell that her dear husband's death had ruined her.

Having embarked upon this task with every intention of telling her children the truth, Emily did not leave out many details, save those that she knew would upset Maddie the most.

She told them of how, though she had cared for them during her every waking moment, she had descended into a spiralling pit of depression, completely shattered by what had happened.

The sky outside was bright now and light streamed in merrily through the windows, contrasting Emily's words.

Glancing at Father Peter briefly as she spoke, their mother told them of how she had sought help from God.

She had known it would not bring Arthur back, for that was impossible, supposedly.

She had just wanted the pain to stop.

It was unbearable.

She couldn't stand it any longer.

"And then I met Richard…" Emily said then, warily, and her voice was flinty and cold, as if the memory was a happy one painted blood red. "I had seen him in the village a few times already…" She continued. "But we had never met. Straight away, I thought my prayers had been answered…"

It was the turn of the old Vicar now to hold an unreadable expression, and as Emily looked across the pews at him, she could not decipher even in the slightest the look on his face.

Then Emily went on to tell them how Richard brought her out of her depression, saving her from her terrible downward spiral, and though she had never stopped loving their real father, she had raised Maddie and Johnathan to believe that Richard was their father, hoping to spare them the same pain.

"But then things started to change…" Emily warned, and again her words hung in the air ominously as if the fate of the universe rested upon them. "The money I had been left by your father, I'd never really used. All of a sudden, Richard began asking to borrow some of it. Only small amounts at first, but it wasn't long before it was much more. I asked him what he was spending it on, but he would never tell me."

"Why did you keep giving it to him then?" Johnathan asked, and indeed it was the most logical question, but the look on his mother's face told him that the answer to his query had been on her next breath.

"One day he asked me again, and this time he asked me for more than he'd ever asked for before. I told him no. I told him I wasn't going to give it to him if he didn't tell me what he was using it for."

Silence hung between the four of them then, and Johnathan knew exactly what was coming next. He clenched his fists and gritted his teeth, preparing for the pain in his chest that he was sure would accompany his mother's words.

"That was the first time he hit me…" She breathed then, her voice scarcely a whisper, and her hand went to her face instinctively as if the pain of the strike still plagued her.

It most definitely plagued Johnathan however, and the sudden assault at his heart knocked every ounce of breath from his body. He felt as though he had been struck square in the chest by a bucking horse, and he wheezed for breath, though he did his best not to let it show.

He imagined it would have been quite difficult to explain.

"What did you do?" He asked, keeping his voice quiet, barely able to get enough air into his lungs to force the words from his tongue.

"What could I do?" His mother asked, shrugging her shoulders, defeated. "He hit me and then took the money anyway. When he came home that night, I'd recovered, and I confronted him about it. He hit me again, and again, and again…" Her voice trailed off and her eyes glazed slightly as her body physically shuddered at the thought.

Clearly this had been going on for a long time.

"He never asked me for money again." Emily whispered then. "He just took it. If I ever said a word, he would beat me. If I ever did anything he didn't like, he would beat me. Before long I learned to keep my mouth shut…"

"Why…?" Johnathan whispered, hit stomach turning at his mother's sorrowful words.

"You and Maddie were still okay…" Emily replied, as if that explained everything. "If I'd tried to leave…I was afraid of what he might do…" She admitted then, clutching Maddie close to her.

She had only ever been protecting her children, even though that had come at such a hefty cost.

Johnathan sighed deeply and pushed himself to his feet, wincing slightly as he moved. He stepped forward and pulled his mother and his sister both into his arms. They all held on tightly and, for a moment at least, everything was alright again.

It was late into morning by now and, regardless of everything that had happened and all that had been revealed, Johnathan's natural instincts kicked in.

His stomach rumbled and growled fiercely and they all laughed, for the first time in far too long.

"You must keep your strength up, Johnathan." Father Peter commented, laughing also, rising to his feet, pleased that their mood was lifting. "I'll fix breakfast for you all."

"Thank you Father." Emily replied gratefully, smiling warmly at him.

The old Vicar was one of the few people who had always been there for her, even if things had grown out of control, and for that she would be eternally grateful.

Suddenly then, jerking and pulling away from her mother and brother, Maddie screamed and pointed with a locked arm across the vast hall and towards the heavy wooden door.

"There!" She screeched, her breaths short and sharp and panicked. "Him! There! He's there!"

"Maddie…Maddie calm down. What is it!?" Johnathan asked, immediately at her side trying to quiet her.

"It's him!" She urged, shaking violently, clinging desperately to her big brother. "Richard! He was there!"

Johnathan's eyes snapped across the room to the doorway. The heavy wooden door was slightly ajar, and there was no sign of movement that he could see. But that didn't matter. Maddie was only very young, but then so was he, and he trusted her implicitly.

"Wait here." He instructed, not really directing his words at any one of them, but rather at them all.

Rising slowly to his feet, eyes trained on the doorway with an unreadable expression painted upon his face, Johnathan led Maddie over to their mother and then made for the door, his poise purposeful and exact, despite his injuries.

"Johnathan…" Emily barely managed, choking back desperate tears. "No…Please…It's too dangerous…"

But when Johnathan turned back to his mother then, fixing her gaze with his own, it was not his eyes that she saw, but instead those of her husband, fierce and committed and determined to protect his family, even from beyond the grave.

"Stay safe Em." Arthur told his wife gently, speaking through his brave son as if they were one and the same person. "I love you."

Chapter Sixteen

Closing the door slowly and silently behind him, the fresh air of the new day was cool against his face, but stung Johnathan's skin where it was urgently trying to heal. He could feel even as he broke into a run the blisters that had already formed were splitting and bleeding.

But that didn't matter for now.

This was something he knew he had to do.

There would not be another chance.

Pain seared through Johnathan's legs as they churned, pounding ever faster on the hard ground as he crossed grass and stone alike. He wasn't sure exactly where he was running to, but his body seemed to be guided all by itself.

He knew that wasn't exactly true, and that it was in fact his father directing him, and it seemed that Arthur knew exactly where to find Richard.

Those he passed followed him with their eyes, shocked at what they saw. One or two of the surprised villagers even called out to the young boy as he burst into view, and then just as quickly vanished again, moving with frightening speed and intensity.

"Johnathan!?" Was all many of them managed before the young Knight was once again out of sight. Nonetheless, his sudden passing filled them with a mixture of curiosity, concern and, admittedly, fear.

Soon enough Johnathan found himself at the water's edge, beside the river that cut through the village like a knife. Or perhaps it was the village that wrapped around the river like a bandage, holding and binding it, compressing and suffocating it.

There he stopped for a moment, considering that thought, gazing down from the riverbank at the water scurrying and cascading past him, free and uncaring: the way nature should be.

Turning east, Johnathan followed the river. Before long he found himself on the outskirts of Riverbrook.

He kept moving.

Beside him the riverbank grew steeper and steeper until eventually it cut away almost at a right angle from the ground upon which he now stood. The drop to the riverbed down below was not far, but it was sheer, and he glanced over the edge casually, looking down expectantly, knowing somehow inherently exactly what he would find.

Sure enough, he was not disappointed, and his cold, steely gaze met Richard's with a fresh, pulsing hatred.

Never in his short lifetime had Johnathan ever viewed another human being with such venomous thoughts, and though it knew such feelings were not decent or proper, he felt that, considering the situation, they were most certainly justified.

As he clambered down to the edge of the riverbank and dropped into the shallow water below, landing with a splash barely half a dozen feet from where Richard stood, a sudden realisation dawned upon him. His eyes widened in horror and his stomach churned terribly as his mind invented and engineered images right before his eyes.

"This is it…" He managed between furious heartbeats raging against his ribs. "This is where you left him…"

"Finally figured it out have you?" Richard sneered in response, smiling evilly at the young boy, burned and battered and ruined before him.

As if in that moment when Johnathan suddenly realised why Arthur had known this was where Richard would come, it was like a door had been opened in his mind, and a thousand thoughts and realisations came suddenly flooding to him.

They had both known this confrontation was coming, and this was the exact spot where Richard had dumped Arthur's body, all those years ago.

"What are you going to do, boy?" Richard sneered, watching as Johnathan dropped into the shallow water from the bank above.

His bravado was false, for he remembered all too clearly the force behind Johnathan's fury that night the boy had confronted him, but he did not want to reveal his fear to a twelve-year-old.

The false father figure had lost too much already to allow that, and now that his attempt on all three of their lives had failed, he was running out of options.

He had only resorted to the fire because he had been backed into a corner. He knew the village would punish him for what he had done, and he couldn't leave. He had no money. All that he had taken from Emily he had already spent.

Besides, now he wanted to kill them.

It was no longer a necessity, but more of a burning desire.

"Why did you do this?" Johnathan demanded, knowing that he wasn't asking just because he wanted to know, but also because he wanted answers for his father.

"I haven't done anything." Richard replied with feigned innocence, but the smirk on his face made Johnathan sick to his stomach.

"Why did you kill my father? Why did you abuse my mother? Why have you done this to my family!?" Johnathan's voice rose to a crescendo until it finally peaked, and even he was not sure it was his own voice or his father's that Richard heard.

"Oh! That!" Richard scoffed. "I thought you were talking about the fire! For you to follow me all this way I thought it would be something serious at least!"

His mocking tone grated at Johnathan's very core, and the young boy had to force himself with all his will not to lunge at the man and choke the life from him, though he did take two involuntary, albeit wary, steps forward.

"Now now, Johnathan…" Richard taunted, smiling. "That's no way to behave. I have raised you, after all…"

"You're a monster." Johnathan growled through gritted teeth, his voice dripping with malice and coated in hate.

"Me!?" Richard cried, feigning shock. "I'm hurt Johnathan." He mocked, grinning cruelly. "I've not made you what you are." He continued. "It's your father's doing that's had you rampaging around attacking people!"

That was it.

Johnathan had heard enough.

Without thinking, he launched himself forward with an angry cry, raising his hands to strike.

But that was exactly what Richard had been waiting for, banking on the boy's inexperience in such matters.

In a flash the cruel man drew a knife from beneath his shirt, smirking, almost laughing even as he did so.

The young boy saw the blade at the last possible moment. It was a large, study kitchen knife, held outstretched and pointing directly at him.

But even as Johnathan saw it, fists raised, body careering forwards, it was too late. He knew he had made a dreadful mistake. His momentum was too great, and he plunged himself on course for the knife to pummel straight into his chest.

'MOVE!' A voice suddenly bellowed in his ears, almost deafening him, and Johnathan lurched violently to one side as if somebody had just kicked him in the ribs. Whatever it was he felt, it hit him so harshly that his whole body was flung into the river, and for a moment, as he gasped to regain his breath, he felt himself drowning.

Panic seized the young boy as icy cold water rushed into his mouth and flooded his gasping lungs.

Within a few moments however, he found his footing on the rock strewn riverbed, and rose slowly from the water, dripping and glimmering in the light of the day, as if he had just been reborn.

His lungs filled with huge gulps of air and his eyes settled immediately upon Richard, level and focused.

Where he stood the water came up to his waist and rushed about him in a freezing cold frenzy, but he ignored it.

He stepped forwards, slowly and purposefully, though his legs fought against the strong current as it tried to pull him back under.

"W…Wha…What…?" Richard stammered, blade still in hand, though his face wore an expression of shock and confusion.

"You caught me off guard." Johnathan warned, his voice slow and controlled, yet still full of anger, though many years of it now. He knew that the words weren't his.

In fact, he wasn't in control now at all. He was aware of what he was doing and what he was saying, but he wasn't actually controlling any of it.

It was as if he was a passenger in his own body.

"I will not allow you to do the same to my son."

"Arthur…?" Richard blurted then, as if seeing the man for the first time, his eyes widening in fear and disbelief.

He still held the knife out before him, but now it trembled in his terrified hand, and all traces of his false confidence had melted away in the presence of this ghost before him, concealed within the body of a boy.

The water level dropped to Johnathan's thighs as he moved and his pace quickened. Suddenly, as if sensing the danger he was in for the first time, Richard snapped to his senses and bolted back up the riverbank.

Had Johnathan not been slowed so by the current, Arthur would have had him there and then, but the water rushed about him still, and he had to fight with all the strength he could muster to break free of it.

By the time the ice cold river was down to mere inches about his feet, Richard had scrambled back up the bank and was bolting away for all he was worth, fleeing in terror from the ghost before him.

As Johnathan clambered up the bank behind him, he only glimpsed the terrible man disappear between the cottages in the distance and vanish from sight.

He sighed deeply and felt the veil lift from him.

His thoughts raced and considered his options. He had very nearly got himself killed.

It was only because of his father that he was still alive, again…

But he didn't have long to think over those thoughts, for after barely even a minute, the young boy gasped suddenly as his muscles seized up as a result of being plunged into the freezing water, and he clutched at his legs in agony.

At least the pain was only temporary, and it was certainly much more convenient than a knife between his ribs would have been.

As if in response to his thoughts, his father's voice sounded again, and now that Johnathan wasn't so rage blind, he could tell that the voice wasn't speaking aloud, but rather speaking directly to him, as if communicating by thought.

'Be careful, Johnathan.' Arthur warned him. 'That man is pure evil. Don't underestimate his wickedness.'

And then his father's voice was gone, replaced only by the sound of his own gasping breaths, and a throbbing in his head so heavy that the young boy felt as though he had been viciously clubbed.

Still, only minutes ago his foolish rage had nearly cost him his life, and he thought rather seriously on that notion as he groaned and climbed to his feet. He began to drag his stiff legs forward and trudged back towards the church, wondering what on Earth to do now.

Once again though, his wonderings lasted only for a brief while, before the wet dressings plastered all across his body began to pull away and tear at his seared skin beneath, and within what felt like only moments, Johnathan was in agony yet again.

Writhing and squirming in his own skin, unable to escape, it was all the young boy could do to race back to Father Peter's church, desperate for aid.

Chapter Seventeen

"Johnathan, what were you thinking!?" Emily demanded, her voice laced with panic while her eyes darted wildly and her arms flailed madly.

Her son did not reply.

He could not. For even as she ranted, Father Peter was removing the shrivelled dressings from Johnathan's arms and legs and torso, and the young boy winced and gritted his teeth against the pain, drawing in deep breaths and exhaling slowly.

The old man peeled back the dressings as carefully as he could. But no matter how cautious he was, they were wet and cold and stuck to Johnathan's wounds like glue, and as they came away, so did a great deal of his skin, both burned and fresh.

The whole ordeal took the best part of an hour. Once all of his dressings had been removed, the extent of Johnathan's wounds became clear.

His skin was bubbled with sticky red and yellow liquid, oozing all over with clear and coloured puss. The sea of injury that had surfaced covered almost all of Johnathan's arms and legs, save the one hand that had been spared, and the vast majority of his back, stomach and chest.

Grimacing as he did so, the old Vicar replaced Johnathan's dressings with fresh ones, washing them over with cool water in the process, knowing the wounds needed to be kept as clean as possible.

If any of them were to get infected, he knew the young Knight would be in serious trouble.

Finally, after what felt like a lifetime, Johnathan sat up as best he could, smiling ruefully in thanks to Father Peter.

"What happened, Johnathan?" His mother asked him. Her voice was much calmer now and her panic had subsided somewhat, though her words still quivered in something that was more likely than not shock.

"That man is evil." Johnathan breathed, as if that was all that need to be said.

Rising slowly to his feet, his skin sore and burning, Johnathan limped over to the pews once again and lowered himself carefully to sit.

"He's a monster." Emily agreed, her voice barely a whisper, looking upon her only son and eldest child as he struggled and fought with his wounds, sorrow and fear gripping her heart.

Richard had done this to her boy.

That man.

That fiend.

"He went to the place on the river where he dumped Arthur's body…" Johnathan continued without the need for prompting.

So desperately did he want to say father, rather than Arthur, but for some reason, after everything that had happened, he just couldn't bring himself to do it.

He sighed mournfully, and that simple sound was filled with such terrible and endless remorse.

Johnathan's mother swallowed a lump in her throat, and her eyes brimmed with tears, threatening to break free at any moment.

Somehow she knew what was coming next.

"He tried to kill me too…" Her son stated, his voice level and steady, cold and emotionless. The simple notion that his voice could hold that tone chilled Emily to the very bone. Guilt suddenly washed over her as she looked upon her son helplessly.

What had she done?

What had she allowed to happen?

Regret and blame swallowed Emily up from the inside as she gazed upon her awful work and all that she had failed to protect. It was no longer only sorrow and grief that consumed her.

"Arthur protected me though…" Johnathan went on, oblivious to his mother's silent and internal torment.

Maddie sidled over to the pew upon which her brother sat, her movements wary, almost even nervous, as if something drastic had changed and she would no longer be welcome beside him.

Johnathan smiled warmly, knowing she was only scared, and held out his arm to her. She smiled a sweet and shy little smile, her eyes young and winnow some, and cradled into him gratefully. She edged close, but not quite touching, not wanting to hurt him, but he smirked and pulled her up against his side, indifferent to the pain, for it was not important.

Maddie's shyness and worry faded away almost instantly and Emily's heart melted at the sight of her children, and things between the three of them were suddenly alright again.

These bouts would undoubtedly continue, at least until something drastic changed, on way or another.

"Do you need anything?" Father Peter asked then, breaking the silence that had fallen over them in that moment of unification.

At those words, after everything they had been through, as will almost always be the case with young men, Johnathan's first thought was, of course, food.

As if on cue his stomach growled loudly and fiercely, feeling rather neglected and calling out desperately to be fed.

They all laughed openly then, for the second time in the same day, and not a word needed to be said.

"I'll lock the door…" Father Peter assured them as he gathered his things, knowing that another visit from Richard would most certainly not be welcomed. "But I'll leave you a key…" He added, rummaging around inside his robe for the spare key he always kept on his person.

Finding it, he smiled as he handed it to Emily Knight, and the gratitude in her eyes said volumes more than words ever could have done.

The door closed quietly and locked with a satisfying click behind the old man as he disappeared outside, and silence once again fell over the vast hall.

Johnathan held his sister close, and their mother sat down beside them, on Johnathan's opposite side, and reached her arms around them both, holding her family near.

There was only one person missing, and, sadly, there was nothing any of them could do to change that.

The day wore on in Father Peter's absence and Johnathan and Maddie and Emily Knight enjoyed the time they were given together, as a family should, and were grateful for whomever it was who had been watching over them.

Johnathan had a good idea who it had been, but he had no way to show his mother or sister all that he had seen.

Words alone would not do it.

Soon enough Father Peter returned, and even as the kind old man set about preparing their food, the beginnings of an idea formed in Johnathan's mind.

Afternoon came and went and they ate the banquet Father Peter prepared for them. There was food enough to feed them several times over, and they laughed and joked and recovered and were the happiest they had been in a long while.

Of course Richard's immediate presence still hung over them all, but for now at least they were safe.

The light of the day streamed in through the high windows and illuminated their day. Visitors came by to see how they were. Before long news of their recovery spread, and it seemed that the whole village appeared on the doorstep at once.

Each and every person was invited in, greeted warmly by the old Vicar, and Emily felt safe with her friends and family all about her, as we all do.

But, nonetheless, regardless of who came and went, regardless of who visited and departed, there was always one face that was forever lost amongst the crowd, and his face was the one she longed to see the most.

Evening encroached upon them and a deep, vast, endless darkness swept in upon the tiny, insignificant village of Riverbrook.

Cold winds cut through the trees and bit harshly at the exposed faces of anybody who dared still remain out under the enormous sky, scattered with an ocean of burned out stars that seethed and watched without a sound.

A million and more shining eyes that had gazed down upon the face of the Earth for a hundred millennia and even longer, turned their cruel eyes now to all that was unfolding before them, and for not the first time in history, something impossible and wonderful, a miracle, began to unfold.

It was then, once all their plates and cups and dishes and bowls from the day had been cleared and cleaned and dried, that Johnathan put his notion into action.

Father Peter fetched them blankets and lanterns and candles, delving every time into his seemingly bottomless storeroom. He offered them beds in his quarters in the church and continually asked if there was anything else they needed.

He was a good man.

There are a few of them left, it would seem, but only a few.

"What is it, Johnathan?" He suddenly asked the young boy, sensing somehow amidst all else that there was something on his mind.

"There's something I need to do first." Johnathan told him, grateful for his perception.

"Yes…?" The old Vicar replied, not quite understanding what the boy needed, but already with that simple reply offering him anything he could possibly give.

Johnathan glanced for a moment across at his mother and sister, and their expressions cast back at him questioningly, wondering what he was doing.

The young boy took a deep breath, unsure whether what he had in mind would even work.

"Please, do you have a mirror?"

Chapter Eighteen

The full length mirror stood directly in the centre of the aisle, between the rows of pews on either side. Framing the perfect, shining face of the mirror that reflected the dancing orange light of the candles upon the high walls of the hall, was an ornately carved, wooden frame. Swirls and twists and patterns that didn't even have names to describe them were etched into the border, sculpted however many years ago with such intricacy and finesse that it left no room for words alone to describe them.

It was clear that this mirror had seen many years in its time, like the one Johnathan had sadly lost to the flames.

Perhaps it was indeed time that wore them down so, but then also that made them so unique and invaluable and, ironically, timeless.

Young Maddie and guilty Emily and the empathetic Vicar looked on, intrigued. Neither Emily nor Father Peter had any idea what the mirror was for.

Maddie, in the back of her mind, knew what Johnathan was going to try to do. He had tried to show he once before, she remembered. He had taken her into his room and shown her his mirror, and had demanded that he'd seen a man in his reflection.

She hadn't understood it at the time, and she still didn't, but she hoped that this time, for her brother's sake, if nothing else, that whatever he was trying to do worked.

He too was unsure.

He had every right to be, he thought.

For one, what he was trying to do sounded impossible in the first place.

Secondly, he was going to try and do it using a different mirror. Whether that made any difference at all or not, he had no idea.

And thirdly…

He wasn't even sure what other reason to choose to make his notion sound even more ludicrous than it already was.

There was bound to be one, he reasoned, and so, considering that, he simply pushed them all from his mind.

The day had long worn into night. Dusk had come and gone silently, and now it was time for him to try.

What else could he do?

He had nothing else.

And so, resolutely, the young boy set him mind to the task at hand.

For a long time Johnathan simply stood. Staring at his own reflection in the mirror, flickering slightly by the hundred or so candles, he bore his eyes into his own gaze, concentrating as hard as he possibly could.

Not really knowing what else to do besides that, to begin with, Johnathan simply hoped the image of what he now knew was his father would appear, and he tried with all his might to simply will the strange phenomenon to be.

But after a while Johnathan had seemingly achieved nothing, and his thoughts had settled upon the single, haunting image of the mist surrounded words that had at the time, and still even now, terrified him.

look after them

The image stuck in his mind and would not budge. After a while he conceded that he wouldn't be able to remove the thought, and so instead he tried to focus on it.

And the more he thought of it, the more it frightened him. But yet, even still, he only focused harder on it.

Then other memories came flooding to him in a sudden great rush, almost drowning him in thought.

He thought of Brock, the bully at school.

He thought of the fire.

He thought of his father.

He tried to picture the strong, brave man he had seen in his silver mirror in his bedroom.

But, hard as he tried, nothing happened.

Silence hung heavily all around, even as his mind raced, and in the end, after everything, Johnathan still found himself staring back at his own frustrated, terrified reflection: young and feeble and small and insignificant.

Eventually, after a full hour of trying, all his efforts in vain, Johnathan sat down upon the hard, stone floor, crossing his legs and resting his elbows on his knees. Dropping his head into his hands he rubbed his weary eyes and groaned, wondering what he was doing wrong.

Wondering what he was even doing.

Emily and Father Peter exchanged a worried look. Still they had no idea what Johnathan was trying to do, and to them it had simply looked like he had spent the past hour staring at his own reflection in silence.

Maddie however, moving on swift and silent steps as if on her very purpose and existence hung the balance of the whole world, rose to her feet and swept to her brother's side all in a single motion.

His head still in his hands, Johnathan did not even know his sister was there until her hand gently grazed his shoulders and back, caressing his concerns with every movement.

She didn't startle him however, and her touch comforted him greatly.

Dropping gracefully to the floor beside him and crossing her legs also, Maddie rested her head lightly upon her brother's shoulder and took up immediate occupancy. She too stared at their slightly smudged reflection in the mirror, waiting for something to happen.

The old Vicar looked on curiously at the pair of them.

He had known them their entire lives, and they had always been so close. Never had a day gone by when they hadn't been there for each other, no matter what. He looked over to their mother once again, exchanging yet another glance, only this one said something completely different to those previous.

Emily looked weary, worried and confused, but she loved her children very much. More than anything, Of course she did. What mother doesn't?

And not only did Father Peter know that for a fact, but it was all too plain to see as she went and sat down with Johnathan and Emily, joining them, placing one arm around each of them.

Turning her eyes to the mirror, Emily also gazed into its face and saw the reflection of the three of them, but, at least at that point, only the three of them.

It was then that Father Peter felt once again the presence that he had felt so often of late, and he smiled warmly at the family before him.

The fight had been long, and it wasn't over yet, but he knew that they deserved this moment more than any, and so he retired to his quarters, ensuring of course on his way that the heavy wooden doors to the church were locked, making certain the Knights' safety, and he pulled the door to his quarters silently shut behind him, giving the four of them their privacy.

Johnathan smiled.

Maddie's eyes widened in wonder.

Emily gasped and choked on a shocked sob.

Arthur looked at the three of them with eyes so full of love and sorrow that it struck at the heart just to see such a thing.

Stood behind her in their reflection, Emily saw the face she had so desperately longed to see for years now. The man she had so badly yearned for was all of a sudden right there before her.

His eyes rested for a moment on their children, and as his gaze swept over Johnathan and his wounds, his expression for a moment became creased with serious concern. But then, after a few seconds, a look of decision crossed the devoted father's face, and all was well again.

Emily whipped her head round expecting to see him stood behind her.

But there was nothing.

Confused, she looked back to the mirror and Arthur smiled warmly at her, though she could see in his eyes the pain that he too felt, and just to know that he missed her just as much as she missed him warmed Emily's broken heart to the core.

His silent reassurance set her worries aside. Suddenly, even after all these years, she knew that he still loved them.

She knew that she had done all she could.

She knew he was proud of her.

Their children were strong and brave and loving.

His unspoken words eased her self-blame and doubt, and for that night, for the first time in far too long, it was as if Arthur was right there with them.

Chapter Nineteen

The next morning Emily Knight awoke and found herself lay on the floor of the church, curled up on one of the blankets that Father Peter had brought them. Her children slept soundly with her, the three of them all huddled together, and even before she had lifted her head, Emily felt a warmth upon her back that she instinctively knew had kept the cold from touching them all throughout the night.

She knew what that warmth was, and though she could not touch him, she smiled contentedly and a single tear of happiness managed to squeeze its way from her grasp, for she knew without a shadow of a doubt that her dear husband, Arthur Knight, was there with them still.

Looking up, Emily squinted slightly against the streaks of bright morning light that flooded the enormous cavern that had been their bedroom for the night.

Beneath her the blanket was soft and warm and she felt almost as if she could stay there quite comfortably forever.

There was not a sound to be heard besides that of the early morning calls of the birds outside. Mrs Knight lay there with her children and her husband and listened to their sound for quite some time.

She had no idea exactly how long really, and quite frankly, she really didn't care.

They were all safe, and their family was whole again.

What else really mattered in the world?

Nothing, she decided, and she sank deeper and deeper into blissful contentment, wrapping her arms ever tighter about her babies, wishing only that Arthur was able to wrap his arms round her in turn.

Sadly, Emily knew there would be no way to bring him back for real. What had already happened was impossible, to ask for that too would be beyond insanity.

Shifting her weight slightly, sliding her arm beneath Johnathan and Maddie as she did so, Emily drew in a sharp breath as she caught one of her son's dressings, accidentally ripping it away from his skin.

Instinctively, with concern that can only be learned as a parent, her attention darted in, half rising in an instant, only stopping because what she saw bewildered her completely.

She ran her fingers over the skin on Johnathan's arm where she had just accidentally pulled the dressing from.

It was smooth and pink and fresh, unharmed and unscarred.

Perfect.

The feeling that filled Emily Knight then was indescribable.

She knew instantly that this was her husband's work, and she whispered a silent prayer thanking him, and telling him that she loved him with all her heart.

As if in response the warmth at her back intensified, and she could even have sworn that she felt the fingers of a hand interlocking with her own.

Of course that was madness, but even as she looked at her empty hand, she felt Arthur's there even still, and smiled affectionately, for she did indeed love him with everything that she had, even if he was gone, never to return.

When Father Peter decided he had allowed them enough time, for now the sun had well and truly broken over the horizon far to the east, he pushed the door to his quarters open and descended into the nave expectantly.

Even before he entered the vast room he was smiling, for he could feel the energy and the love emanating from within.

The sight that beheld him took even his breath away however.

All three of the Knights, Johnathan, Maddie and Emily, were awake, and he could certainly feel the presence of a fourth within, even if he could not see him, he knew Arthur was there.

Emily was just peeling off the last of Johnathan's dressings, revealing in fact that every inch of his wounds had completely healed overnight. Such a thing the old man knew was impossible, but even as the young boy checked and double checked to ensure he hadn't missed something, Father Peter knew that where the Knights were concerned, there was no such thing.

"Well…" The old Vicar greeted them, smiling widely and openly, lifting his hands, palms upwards, simply because he had no idea what to say.

Emily smiled warmly at him and Maddie laughed with delight and threw herself at her brother, holding him closely, overjoyed at his miraculous recovery.

It appeared that many miracles were taking place here.

Undoubtedly, this would not be the last.

"Good morning Father…" Johnathan greeted the old man, nodding his head and smiling, though there was the glint of perhaps a more serious look in his eye, and the hint of a more meaningful note in his tone.

Somehow then, imperceptibly, the old Vicar realised that the young boy hadn't simply greeted him, but he had also greeted Arthur Knight, his real father, and that notion was, to say the very least, momentous.

"Good morning Johnathan…" He replied, revealing by his tone that he understood the significance of what had just happened.

The moment was lost on Emily and Maddie, but that didn't matter. What mattered most was that it had happened, and that now, after much time and preparation, Johnathan was finally ready.

For the most part the preparations hadn't even been his own, but at least now he had finally accepted his fate.

Many people work in many mysterious ways.

"Will you be sitting in on the Sunday Service?" Father Peter asked then, and again his tone spoke volumes. It suggested that he thought, for reasons completely unknown to Emily, that it was perhaps a very good idea for them to attend.

She looked at him with one eyebrow raised, questioningly, but he had no answers for her, and could give her nothing other than the hopeful expression he already held.

"I don't see why we shouldn't…" Emily started, worried perhaps that the old Vicar was trying to warn her of something.

But Maddie piped up before he could say any more.

"Will it be safe?" She asked meekly, thinking immediately of all that had happened recently, and how easily Richard would be able to slip into the church amongst the crowds.

However, it was not Emily or Father Peter who replied, as you might have expected, but instead it was her brother, Johnathan.

"It will be the safest place in the whole village." He assured his little sister, pacing over and placing his arm around her tiny shoulders.

She smiled up at him thankfully.

"Everyone will be here…" Her brother continued, looking around the vast, empty hall as if they already were. "Everyone…" He repeated then, quite meaningfully, turning his gaze to his mother and Father Peter for a brief moment.

Emily's breath snatched for a second at the sight of the ferocity in her son's eyes. But it was not an evil she saw within him.

Instead it was a will and a drive like none she had ever seen.

In fact, that wasn't entirely true.

She had seen such a look before, but only ever in the eyes of one other person.

Her dear husband.

Her dear Arthur Knight.

Chapter Twenty

The spiral staircase wound its way up into the darkness ominously, and with the echoing sound of Johnathan's own footsteps reverberating round as he climbed. The troubled young boy felt his way through the blackness, for he had not brought any kind of light with him, and all the while he thought on his sins.

If any of us were to think too hard and too long about such a thing, our day would undoubtedly ensue to be a very gloomy one indeed.

Sin is a strange thing, and many consider some certain desires and actions to be sinful, whilst others do not.

Surely then, considering that notion, what qualifies as a sin and what does not, is merely a matter of opinion.

And if the argument were to be made that those things considered sinful are depicted by a man's God, whomever that might be at the time, then surely it is simply a question of who has the strictest imaginary friend?

Nonetheless, ignoring the ethics of the situation, the young Knight's thoughts as he ascended the twisting stairs in the cold, pitch black, were melancholy indeed.

Finally, after what felt like many long, hard, torturous years, be broke through the darkness, and was bathed in glorious light as he reached the top of the winding staircase.

Immediately present above him was the church's enormous bell. It was massive and hung perilously from the thickest rope Johnathan had ever seen. Somehow, in that moment, it seemed as if the bell had been forever in existence, and that time had for all eternity been measured by its huge, steady ring, echoing out across the world.

Looking out then, Johnathan's gaze swept across the tiny village of Riverbrook that he had for his whole life called home, and then even further, for the bell tower was high and he could see for miles and miles in every direction.

The incandescent morning sun bathed the land in all its glory and the fields glowed rich and ripe and golden.

It was certainly a sight to be beheld.

He had never before witnessed this view. In fact, most hadn't, and the young boy felt most privileged. Considering for a moment racing back down the stairs to fetch his mother and sister, so that he could share this with them, Johnathan very nearly turned on his heel.

But then, for some reason, he didn't. He knew he was already sharing it with someone, and he turned instinctively then to see his father standing beside him.

The great man looked so real that Johnathan was convinced that if he reached out he would even be able to touch him. And then, without even a thought from him, Johnathan's arm automatically stretched out, and his hand brushed gently, warily even, against Arthur's rough, worn leather jacket, faded and battered.

His father smiled warmly and his dark eyes enveloped Johnathan caringly in their gaze.

Hope soared within the young boy.

"You know this is it…" He said then, his rich, coarse voice breaking the perfect silence at least as dramatically as the huge bell above might have done, warning even in its very tone.

Johnathan sighed, looking out at the golden meadows once more.

"I thought it might be…" He replied mournfully. "What's going to happen?" He asked his father then, looking back to where he stood.

"I honestly don't know son…" Arthur replied, his voice harrowed by sadness and regret.

"You mean anything could happen?" Johnathan almost cried, of course, as is human nature, imagining the worst.

"I will protect you." Arthur replied, quite seriously, then. "But you must protect your mother and your sister."

Without a moment's hesitation, Johnathan nodded in agreement.

"I will." He promised firmly, knowing and truly believing, without a shadow of a doubt, that his father would protect him to the very end.

"I know you will son." Arthur replied warmly, and his words filled Johnathan with a feeling that he had, without even realising it, longed for, for all his life.

It was the feeling that a son can only attain from his father, and without such a precious bond, much is lost along the way.

Chapter Twenty One

It was a strange feeling that engulfed Emily Knight that Sunday morning as the day began to wear on and take all those who lived in the village of Riverbrook, and indeed also all those who lived in the world, down their inexorably fated paths.

She didn't know whether or not in fact that was true.

Was there such a thing as fate?

But it didn't matter what she knew.

All that mattered was that it was what she believed.

Whatever happened, or didn't happen for that matter, was supposed to. And in the end, one way or another, it would eventually always lead them on to where they needed to be.

Her bizarre mood seemed to emanate out from her as people filed slowly and dutifully and hopefully in to the church, and as it spread and touched each and every soul who walked through the huge, heavy wooden doors, the vast hall was filled with a pensive and expectant air.

Expectant of what, exactly, she wasn't sure. But the brooding look on Father Peter's face, combined with the fierce and focused expression that her son held, sat beside her still somewhat anxious daughter, filled Emily with a mixture of emotions so strange that she realised all at once that in fact she had absolutely no idea how she felt.

Almost as if everything that had happened of late was coming round full circle, as Father Peter stepped up to the dais at the front on the nave, set at the very centre of the pews, a chill ran up and down her spine.

Déjà vu tickled her every nerve, taunting her, and she swallowed nervously as the old man took a deep breath ready to speak.

"Good morning my friends…" He began, smiling, spreading his arms wide in an open and welcoming manner, as he always did, and immediately captivating his audience.

Unmatched, his presence filled the enormous room and grasped every attention in an instant.

However, no matter how captivated his audience was, there were still a few who could not resist the odd glance, even if just for the briefest moment, over at Johnathan and Maddie and Emily.

The Davies' attendance at the Service had caused quite a stir, and especially considering Johnathan's condition.

Or perhaps, more accurately, his lack of poor condition.

It was fairly safe to say that everybody had noticed his seemingly miraculous recovery. But, shocking as it may have been, it seemed the topic was too alarming to mention, and nobody, not one soul, had brought it up. Whether they were too polite, or afraid, or perhaps perplexed to ask, Johnathan didn't mind, for he quite purposefully declined to bring it into conversation either, and that suited him just fine.

And so it had transpired that all who had greeted him, wild-eyed and baffled, had simply asked him how he was, and not once mentioned his injuries, or more so lack of.

"I'm pleased to have you all here this fine day..." Father Peter continued, motioning expressively with his hands as he spoke towards the sunshine that poured in through the high windows, illuminating the crowd sat so eagerly before him.

Even though the huge beams of light swallowed the people of Riverbrook so, a hundred and more candles were still lit for the Service, for this was traditional and good and proper, and Father Peter always ensured that it was so.

He looked then quite purposefully and directly at Emily, catching her gaze, though his eyes seemed to engulf Johnathan and Maddie also.

"As you are all aware, we are very lucky to have Emily and Maddie and Johnathan in our presence today."

His words were full of sincerity and his voice was thick with emotion. It was almost as if the old man knew something that his audience didn't.

Or, perhaps, he was just overwhelmed by the whole situation.

"Today, my friends, I would like to talk about something that I think we all need to hear..."

He pressed on, barely pausing for even a second.

"For I think this has been building for a very long time..."

His voice wavered slightly and the light that streamed in through the windows dimmed for a moment, but then immediately brightened again.

Hesitating for a second then, the old man's brow furrowed deep in thought. He cast a brief glance around the room, and after a minute or two his gaze settled and his eyes focused on a single point.

He nodded as if in acknowledgement, although he seemed not to be looking at anybody in particular.

Then he took a deep breath and spoke again.

"People come to see me for many different reasons…" He began again, his voice pensive. "And such is my purpose…" He admitted, opening his hands in acceptance, palms upwards.

Maddie looked up and her brother sat next to her and he smiled warmly.

"Some people need help…" The old Vicar went on. "Many seek advice…" He pursed his lips slightly. "Others want forgiveness…"

Somehow, even though Father Peter's words seemed strange to most, Johnathan thought he knew what was coming next. In fact, there was no thought about it, he knew for a fact what the old man's next breath would reveal.

"But it doesn't matter what they come to see me for…" The Vicar continued ominously, pausing for mere moments once more. "The reason behind their visits is always the same…"

It was as if the pews themselves were holding their breath, and the nave was filled to the brim with anticipation, hanging on his every word in maddening suspense.

"Demons…" He breathed then, as if on that single word had escaped everything he had been holding back. "Most people fear their demons, for they embody their deepest, darkest sins, and in their fear they turn to me for guidance…"

Anxiety rippled through his audience, for somehow their suspense still had not faded.

"But some people, though only the bravest of us, turn to face them alone. And in times of great adversity, when their pain and their suffering is at its worst, these few are driven only to become stronger, fighting with evermore fire and evermore resolve."

The faces of his audience before him were bleak, as his words hit them like a dreadful hurricane.

He pressed on.

"Some try to hide from their demons, or dress them as something else entirely. But disguising them doesn't work. Only you know what they truly are. And you may be able to run from them for a while, but they will be kept at bay only for so long. You cannot escape from them."

The tone of the old Vicar's voice was so serious and deathly level that a chill ran through his audience like a rippling tsunami, and he paused for breath and to survey the effect of his words, but just for a moment. Unfaltering, the wave of disaster caused by his devastatingly accurate words continued.

"Who amongst you has faced your demons!?" He demanded then, scanning the faces of his crowd with piercing eyes. He was not accusing any single person, far from it. But his words were stirring the people of Riverbrook, and preparing them for something that they did not even realise was coming.

Though his gaze was penetrating, he did not linger on any one soul.

Perhaps his eyes had not found the one they sought.

"He who can honestly stand proud and face that which he fears most about himself, is a good man indeed…" The Vicar's tone changed then, dropping and softening, seemingly changing the very atmosphere in the room along with it, as if he had complete and utter control over everybody in his presence.

He sighed deeply then, almost in acceptance.

"That is what makes us stronger and better people…" He said, though his words now sounded mournful, regretful even. "But that is not what makes great men…" He breathed, shaking his head slightly. "That is something else entirely…"

Then, suddenly, the light streaming in through the windows darkened and the day turned almost to night. Clouds swarmed together above the church in a great, angry, seething mass, looming over it evilly.

A monstrous flash of unexpected lighting lit up the blackened sky like an enormous whip, followed immediately by the ominous rumble of thunder.

Wind began to howl terribly outside, attacking the sturdy walls of the church, and though it could not break through the protective stone, the candles that were now the only source of light in the vast hall flickered and waved in fear.

The next flashes and cracks and rumbles of the brewing storm were followed by an immediate and torrential downpour, spitting raindrops the size of a man's clenched fist. The falling water attacked and barraged the church roof and walls endlessly, as if it hated them with a venom so deep that it ran through countless generations.

Then, abused and battered so by the raging storm, the heavy, wooden doors of the church at the opposite end of the nave to where Father Peter stood swung wide open with a loud bang.

Beyond them the storm seethed in eerie blackness that had engulfed the day, like a powerful predator stalks and hunts and overwhelms its prey.

Calmly, Father Peter stepped down from his dais and proceeded up the aisle between the pews towards the door and the treacherous storm.

An icy cold wind rushed in as he approached, trying to push him back and blowing out half of the candles lighting the room.

But he resisted, forcing his way forwards still.

He glanced outside, though he could see barely anything, for it looked almost like the dead of night.

Reaching the large doors, he pushed them to, endeavouring with all his might to lock out the unwanted cold and evil attempting to assault and engulf this sacred place.

But, as if often the way, it always fights its way in somehow, whether by subtlety and guile, or simply by brute force.

Unfortunately, on this occasion, it settled for the latter.

Just as he pushed the doors to, so close to sealing and locking them completely to ensure they didn't swing open again, what dim light there still was outside beyond the old man, was blocked out completely.

In one moment there was nothing but the storm, and in the next there stood before the Father a wiry, shadowy figure that looked over his short frame menacingly, towering above him and seeming to overcome him completely.

The wind and the rain and the thunder and the lightning all seemed to cease then, even if only for a moment, and there hung in the air nothing but a terrifying silence.

The two figures, one illuminated by the candles, and one darkened by the dread night that had descended upon them, stood and stared at each other unmoving and locked in place, as if they had been there for all eternity.

Father's Peter's audience held their breath, but no one dared move.

Finally, drawing up his will and his courage to break the dreadful and ominous silence, Father Peter spoke in a voice that held not a trace of fear whatsoever.

Instead, his words were accepting and understanding, compassionate and caring, and even forgiving and regretful, all at once.

His tone held a hint of finality to it, and even as he spoke, Johnathan felt something building inside of him that was desperate to break free, and for some reason, this time, he chose not to fight it.

"Have you finally come to repent your sins, my son?"

Chapter Twenty Two

The shadowy silhouette surged silently forward and barged straight into the elderly Vicar, forcing him back without a sound. Water sprayed in all directions from the struggle, as the dripping wet shadow knocked Father Peter violently to the ground and, carried by its own momentum, sprawled down on top of him.

Even before the soaking wet figure, robed entirely in black, climbed to its feet, the pool of rainwater that seemed to pour from its saturated clothes, mixed on the floor with a thick pool of blood, swirling red and black and viscous on the cold stone floor of the church.

Rising slowly to stand, the figure revealed its face for the first time, separating slowly from the blackness.

Richard.

His eyes looked wild and crazed as he glanced around, his head jerking left and right in a paranoid frenzy. Mixed with that crazy expression, was a deeper, much more subtle hint of something else entirely.

Something focused and determined and decidedly evil.

Below him, between his feet, lay the body of Father Peter. A blade protruded from his chest, bloodied and bent, and his eyes were closed, never to reopen.

Even in death, the look upon Father's Peter pale face was sympathetic and understanding, as if forgiveness had already been granted.

Richard's expression changed then, and the wild eyed look he'd had about him faded and receded, replaced by something that came from much deeper within him: from his very core.

Now he looked around harshly, seemingly uncaring of the corpse that lay at his feet, and that subtle hint of evil that had just about been present before now surfaced entirely, and bathed him in the full darkness of its menace.

His gaze settled upon Johnathan.

The young boy was stood in the very centre of the aisle, in almost the exact spot where Father Peter had begun delivering his Service, only a few paces further forward.

How he had gotten there, nobody knew.

Somehow he had stood up, without even Maddie or Emily noticing, and positioned himself ready for this moment, and the unwavering look on his face suggested that he had known all along that it would come down to this.

"JOHN!!" Maddie cried desperately, leaping to her feet and almost throwing herself across the pews towards her brother.

Panic gripped her, for even she knew what was coming next.

"Maddie! NO!!" Emily cried, racing after her daughter and rushing to her son's side also.

But when they reached him, they knew not what to do.

The two of them cowered next to Johnathan in the aisle, as fear rippled through the church like a disease, moving with a mind of its own.

Suddenly, feeling the dread and sensing the imminent danger, feet began to scuffle and scrape, voices began to murmur and hearts began to race. The crowd was preparing to flee.

"Wait!" Johnathan's voice commanded them then, and instantly his aura was present, overwhelming everything else, and as is such, his command was automatically obeyed.

The murmurs stifled and the scuffles ceased, though the racings hearts did not quieten.

Nonetheless, all remained where they were, bound by the young boy's command.

Fight, flight, or freeze.

They had already done the latter.

Johnathan had just forbidden the second.

All that remained was the first.

And he was most certainly ready for it.

Arthur Knight had been preparing for this moment for a very long time.

Johnathan did not cower. He was not afraid, and it was all too clear to everybody in the huge hall that something was changing within him. It was something vast and great and powerful, yet also unseen, all at the same time.

He leant down and kissed his wife on the forehead, and then in turn his daughter also, catching each of their gazes for but a mere moment, but once more speaking volumes in those brief exchanges.

Rising slowly to his feet, Johnathan strode forward, his pace measured, meaningful, and purposeful.

His eyes fell upon the bloodied body of Father Peter as he moved, swift and silent as the darkness. Then his gaze swept fleetingly over the throngs to his left and right, all at once taking in their fearful faces, but at the same time seeing nothing.

Finally, settling upon their prize, his eyes bore upon his false father Richard, seeing everything now.

The blood on his hands shone and glimmered in the light of the candles still lit, and the evil grin on his face filled Johnathan with a rage so deep that it could not possibly have been his own.

He was too young to even know such anger.

No, this belonged to his father.

His real father.

Now, finally, he understood, and he looked upon the malevolent face of his demon with eyes afresh.

To his onlookers, as Johnathan strode forwards, it seemed to them that in one stride, in one moment, he was a boy, and yet in the next, he was a full grown man. He seemed to flicker between the two so rapidly, and their figures were so interchangeable, that they were eventually indeed simply one and the same person.

No veil overwhelmed the young boy now.

Not like before.

Instead, he stood proudly alongside his father, standing with him, and it was as if his rage and his fire was coming from deep within of himself.

Stopping short of Richard, and Father Peter's body, by about six full paces, Johnathan, or Arthur, it was impossible to tell from one moment to the next, drew himself up to his full height, standing tall and immovable.

"I am Johnathan Knight." He stated, and in an instant the flickering suddenly stopped, and it was clearly Johnathan who stood against his demon. "My father is Arthur Knight, a better man than you could ever hope to be, and you murdered him in cold blood."

His voice and his presence radiated beyond belief, and was altogether overpowering. The sound of it even seemed to knock Richard aback somewhat, though his malicious expression and intent remained unchanged.

There was shocked silence in the room, aside from a few sharp intakes of breath. Hushed murmurs began again, but Johnathan only had to raise his hand slightly and they instantly quieted.

Johnathan received no words in reply, but the wicked grin that spread even wider across Richard's face said all that words could not.

The demon reached his bloodied hand down toward Father Peter's body, his movements consumed wholly by some evil that neither Johnathan nor Arthur could possibly find words to describe.

They only knew that it was their responsibility to face this demon, and remove it from this world, knowing that if they did not, the further harm it would cause would be matched only by the terrible sins it had already committed.

Richard clasped his hand around the handle of the blade protruding up from between Father Peter's ribs, and slowly drew the knife edge out from the Vicar's dead body, scraping metal against bone terribly as he did so, making a horrible grinding sound that churned the stomach of every onlooker.

He stood then and faced Arthur and Johnathan.

The impossible flickering began again, now that Johnathan's words had been spoken, and in the same space as the young boy appeared Arthur once more.

Richard looked confused for a second.

In one moment, he was looking at a boy, and then in the next, he was looking at a man he had already murdered.

After a few seconds, unable to focus, it even seemed as though they were one and the same person, and then in another it seemed as if they stood side by side.

He didn't know what to make of it, but then, it didn't really matter.

His thoughts were suddenly blurred with rage and frenzy and panic; he would simply kill them both.

He stepped forward callously over Father Peter's cadaver and stood off against Johnathan and Arthur, blood dripping still from the blade in his hand, staining the stone floor at his feet a deathly crimson.

Every footstep Richard took left the wet trail of footprints behind him, for he was still soaked from the rain. Their mark and their meaning was almost as bad as the blood that trickled beside them, mixing the blood of the Earth with that of man, consuming all demons in one great swirling mass, all caught up within that single moment.

Johnathan and Arthur both knew that now this was it.

The time had come.

It was now or never.

They welcomed their enemy, their demon, their great evil.

Their wills and their voices united as one, merging together, casting their ominous sound out to their enemy, ready to strike down the worst of their demons, or to die trying.

Either way, they would not be defeated.

"So be it."

Chapter Twenty Three

For a moment there was silence, but only for a moment, before it was broken by Richard's shrill scream as he charged forward the last three paces to Johnathan and Arthur.

Lunging forward with the blade he held, gripping it with both hands, he drove the point straight towards the boy's exposed chest.

And not for the first time.

But the man expected this, and expertly evaded the attack, stepping deftly aside and kicking Richard hard in the side of his knee as he flurried past.

The evil man's scream of fury turned into a shriek of agony as his knee buckled inwards with a gruesome crunch and he crumpled to the floor, carried forward by his own momentum.

He sprawled to the ground and rolled to his back, baring his teeth and growling like some sort of wild animal, expecting an immediate attack. But Johnathan and Arthur simply stood there, watching, their forms somehow existing in the same space simultaneously.

It was clear to them that Richard was losing his sanity, or perhaps had already lost it, in one form or another.

But regardless, the decision had already been made. His actions and his intentions were unspeakable; he was a demon that needed to be stopped, save endangering anybody else.

Richard clambered to his feet, but unable to support any weight on his one ruined knee, he hobbled precariously on one foot, barely able to balance to stand.

Nonetheless, still he came for them.

Swinging his blade wildly in every direction now, though only throwing himself more off balance with every sweeping movement, his eyes were crazed and seemingly now devoid of anything that vaguely resembled human intelligence. He had devolved entirely into the demon that occupied his soul.

Johnathan and Arthur both saw that it was time, and undoubtedly everyone else in the vast church could feel the presence all around change yet again.

Leaping from his one foot, pushing off with his good leg, the demon bore down upon the young boy once again, this time driving all of his weight behind the blade, cascading down unstoppably.

But then, of course, as had been his fatal mistake from the very beginning, he was not facing a boy, but instead a man, and with the strength of his father, Johnathan caught the demon mid-flight. Clasping his left hand around the wrist in which Richard held the blade, and catching his neck with his right hand, his right arm outstretched, he halted the evil man's plummeting descent with an abrupt jerk.

He held him there for a moment or two, raised high above his own head, suspended by the vice grip Johnathan had about his throat.

The demon gazed down at the young boy with hatred in its eyes, but it was not the boy that it saw now, finally, but instead the man. The man that it loathed with all its soul.

But, hard as he tried, the demon could not move.

It simply did not have the strength to battle this boy, this man, this ghost, this angel, whatever he was, somehow impossibly risen from the dead.

Eventually the blade slipped from his loosening grip as his body slowly failed him, gasping desperately for air that it could not find.

A demon though he might have been, he still had only the body of a feeble human, and without air, that body became useless.

Richard's death was not swift. Nor was it painless. And neither Johnathan nor Arthur took much pleasure in watching the man's life fade away.

They felt every last ounce of breath drain from his body within their grasp, and it sickened them to the stomach.

But, soon enough, the deed was done.

Releasing their vice grip, Richard's lifeless body collapsed to the floor at Johnathan's feet.

The young boy stood there looking down at what he had done for a moment, with absolutely no remorse whatsoever.

Arthur looked down too, his task finally complete, and it was clear to everyone all around the terrible weight that had been lifted from his shoulders.

But with that final success, as is often the way, came also great loss and sacrifice. For with every second that passed, Arthur's presence became less, his aura reducing, and Johnathan's sole presence replaced it, filling the space that his father had occupied for so long now.

Finally, when it was done, the young boy turned and walked over to Father Peter's body, all trace of his real father gone.

Crouching down beside it, he placed a hand on the Vicar's shoulder, in way of a silent thank you; not simply for what he had done for them in those few days, but indeed what he had done for them for their entire lives.

It seemed that there had only ever been two men who had always looked out for Emily and her family, and now they were both dead.

Johnathan rose to his feet with steadfast resolution and an unfaltering resolve.

Now that task fell to him, and he swore silently to both his true father, and to Father Peter, that he would uphold that task as long as there was a single breath left in his body.

He was a Knight after all, and so long as he lived, nothing in the world would stop him from protecting his family.

Chapter Twenty Four

In the months and years that followed that fateful day, who is to say what would have been the normal way for Johnathan and Maddie and Emily to go on?

Should they just continue with their lives as if nothing happened?

Should they mourn the loss of Arthur and Father Peter, and never move on with their own lives?

They didn't know.

I don't think anybody really ever does.

All they did know, was that Arthur had saved them, and undoubtedly countless others.

Johnathan missed his presence greatly.

Of course Emily did too, and Maddie longed fervently that she could have known her real father, but neither of them had shared their very presence with Arthur's, and Johnathan felt decidedly empty in his absence.

For a long time Johnathan retreated into himself somewhat, struggling desperately to cope with the situation. And even, for a time, it seemed to the young boy that there was no way to escape the great cavern that had been left behind inside of him.

His only saving grace was his family.

He lived for them now, doing everything he could for them to protect them and care for them and keep them safe.

Indeed, he most certainly did look after them, just as his father had asked.

Soon enough they had built a new home, with help of course from the rest of the village.

Father Peter was given a most respectful funeral, and buried in the grounds of his church, so that he may remain there for the rest of time, until the end of days.

And so life went on.

As it always does.

Time is indifferent of the events and triumphs and tragedies of mankind, and really even, for the most part, of its own inexorable passage.

But then, one day, completely out of the blue, something changed, once again shifting the lives of the Knights in an entirely new and unexpected direction.

Emily sat at home, as she often did, cleaning and cooking and sewing, trying as hard as she possibly could to keep her mind occupied. But no matter how hard she tried, for some reason, on that particular day, she could not drive the memories of her dear husband from her thoughts.

As much as she loved him, and my word did she love him, those thoughts did all they could to drive her insane. The knowledge that these things that she remembered were done and gone and dead and buried, sought to ruin her, she was sure of it.

Most of the time the only thing that kept Emily going was her children, and even then, much of the time she also tried desperately to remember Father

Peter's words from his Services, for they helped to keep her on track.

'Though at times, my friends, I know it may feel like it's all too much: like there's simply no way to handle the difficult days. But I assure you, with all my heart, that there are always better times ahead.'

That specific reading Emily remembered particularly well, and sometimes it helped. She just hoped that the understanding old man had been right.

'The demons that haunt you today, will be your liberation tomorrow. This I can sorely promise you.'

Johnathan and Maddie were out running errands for her.

At the very least, she was glad that her children had each other for company, for sometimes the long days grew unbearable. Almost to the point where they were simply too difficult to endure.

The front door to their new home, another thatched cottage, suddenly opened, and her son, Johnathan, strode in, a haunted look in his eyes.

Sadly, she was used to that look now, for Johnathan had worn it ever since the day Father Peter had been killed. Although, she suspected, that wasn't the only thing that troubled her dear son.

"Mother?" He said then as he entered, his tone worried and his eyes everywhere. "What's wrong?" He asked, seeing her slumped in a chair at the dining room table, her head in her hands.

"Nothing, Johnathan, thank you…" She lied, unconvincingly, feigning a smile, though again, with relatively meagre success.

Her still loving son, though now he was fifteen years of age, and most certainly in that difficult stage of life where he was not quite a man, but not precisely a boy either, just as Father Peter had predicted, pursed his lips slightly for a moment.

He knew she was lying.

But, unfortunately, he also knew exactly what was wrong. He felt the same thing every day, and he knew there was nothing he could do about it.

Sighing deeply and regretfully, Johnathan leaned down and placed his arms gently around his mother's neck, and she reached up to embrace her son, warmed by his love.

The front door was still open behind Johnathan, and Maddie had not yet followed him in, though neither of them had noticed.

As a matter of fact, she was stood only just outside, her hand lifted up above her face to shield her eyes from the blinding sun, and her eyes desperately trying to focus upon the figure approaching her from the end of their front garden.

"John...? Mother...?" Her voice drifted in from outside, barely even reaching their ears, and not once did she take her eyes from the figure walking slowly towards her, becoming no clearer in the blinding light of the day.

Her heart began to race and barraged furiously against her chest.

"Johnathan!!" She suddenly yelled, filling her lungs and forcing the sound from her tiny frame like an explosion.

Within barely seconds her brother was dutifully at her side.

"Maddie!?" He responded automatically.

Their mother followed him out, only a moment behind him.

"What's wrong!?" She gasped, her breath taken away by fear.

Immediately Johnathan saw the figure of the man and placed himself between Maddie and the threat.

He too however, was forced to lift his hand to his eyes to shield them from the sun, and he could not make out any more than the outline of the person stood before him.

"Who are you!?" He demanded.

Though perhaps it was not the politest way to greet a stranger, Johnathan now favoured more with wariness than manners, be that a good thing or a bad thing, and he waited impatiently for a reply.

But his answer came soon enough, and as the few scattered, drifting clouds high up above them sauntered in front of the blinding sun, dimming its light for perhaps a minute or two, the figure before them came fully into view, and they saw that he was not a stranger after all.

He was tall and broad and looked even at first glance very strong. His dark hair and eyes were set about his chiselled face in a most handsome and attractive way, and he wore a smile that greeted the three of them warmly, and with many years' worth of love lost to the ages.

And because the day was warm and sunny and late into August, his weathered, brown leather jacket, faded and well worn, as it seemingly always had been, was slung casually over his shoulder.

Finally, he was home.

Ross Turner

Thank you for reading Voices in the Mirror

I hope you enjoyed it

Look out for

The Redwoods - Book One

Young Vivian Featherstone comes from a long line of
Lords and Ladies, and her family's seat of
unquestionable influence, wealth and power is owed
to a much treasured heirloom, passed down from
generation to generation.
But when little Vivian, only eleven years of age,
narrowly escapes a plot by a rival, feuding family to
eliminate the Featherstones, she finds herself lost in
the mysterious Redwood Forest.
With assassins pursuing her, and strange and
dangerous creatures all around, can Vivian survive?
And will she discover the power of her family's
heirloom before it's too late?

The Redwoods Rise and Fall - Book Two

Vivian has returned to Virtus, she has defeated the
Greystones, and the once great city even seems to be
well on the way to recovery. But something isn't
right. Vivian feels stranded amongst all that she has
fought to gain, and suffered so terribly to lose. And

now it seems there are new threats and dangers, stemming from old evils. Just as all those before her have either succeeded or succumbed, now she too must face her own rise and fall.

Or

Marcii - Book One of The Dreadhunt Trilogy

For her entire life, raised in the brimming town of Newmarket, all Marcii Dougherty has known is the hustle and bustle of trade and commerce. Entirely concealed amidst the buzz of the market stalls, yet somehow blatantly obvious at the same time, something is dreadfully wrong. Cattle and townsfolk alike are being slaughtered in the depths of the night and their bloodied remains left strewn about for all to see.

Tyran, a man with questionable motives, has elevated himself to the position of Newmarket's saviour. Now Mayor, he has the power to do as he pleases. Using fear as his weapon, he convinces the people of Newmarket that witches are responsible for the attacks. Although innocent, those who stand accused of summoning evil spirits to plague the town have no hope against Tyran's ever growing army.

The furious young Dougherty finds herself utterly helpless to do anything, as Tyran delivers his dreadful justice. But, when one of her dearest friends is found guilty of witchcraft, Marcii can't help but try to intervene, no matter the consequences.

Voices in the Mirror

Please visit my facebook and twitter pages for the latest updates

Ross Turner Books
@RossTurnerBooks

www.rossturnerbooks.com

Printed in Great Britain
by Amazon